Aren't You the One Who...?

by Frances A. Miller

Atheneum   1983   New York

To my own Best Brothers
Sam, Ted, Fred, and John

And to Kirsten, John, Dana, and David
with love

LIBRARY OF CONGRESS CATALOGING IN PUBLICATION DATA

Miller, Frances A.
Aren't you the one who—.

Sequel to: The truth trap.
SUMMARY: With all of his immediate family dead,
sixteen-year-old Matt, living under the shadow of
his sister's murder, finds welcome and
rejection in unexpected places.
I. Title.
PZ7.M61355Ar   1983   [Fic]   82-13798
ISBN 0-689-30961-9

Published simultaneously in Canada by
McClelland & Stewart, Ltd.
Composition by American Book–Stratford Graphic Services,
Brattleboro, Vermont
Printed and bound by Fairfield Graphics,
Fairfield, Pennsylvania
First Edition

83 02854

Aren't You
the One Who . . . ?

1

Morning sunlight dappled the gray paneled walls of Matt's bedroom, bringing out the slight greenish tint that reminded him of old barns and apple orchards and gave him the feeling that he was out of doors, not confined by the four walls. Every morning that he woke up in this room the Ryders had given him, he knew he was a very lucky guy. If it hadn't been for the lieutenant and Sally—and Tony Prado—he'd be in a prison or a mental institution right now, staring at white walls and barred windows with no hope of escape—

Knock it off, McKendrick, he told himself abruptly. One of the all-time great days of your life is about to begin, and you're lying around in bed mooning about something that's ancient history. Forget it. Like Ryder says, it's over and done with. This is Get-the-Cast-Off Day, so get yourself up and celebrating.

It was also his sixteenth birthday, but no one else knew that. When you're a guest in someone's house, you don't drop hints about your birthday and force them into making a big deal out of it whether they want to or not. Getting his leg liberated from the itching cast was going to be all the celebration he needed. As soon as the leg was free, he was heading straight for the Ryders' pool, and tomorrow he'd start serious training, trying out the leg with an easy run at first—No, not tomorrow. It would have to be the day after. Tomorrow he was up with the sun, going home to Craigie, Idaho, for the first time since he and Katie had run away. Something else he didn't want to think about. Not right now, anyway.

With a gleeful whoop, Matt flung himself out of bed and into his shirt and pants. The smell of bacon cooking told him that Mrs. Bly, the Ryders' grandmotherly housekeeper, was in the kitchen before him as usual and busy with breakfast.

"Morning, Mrs. B," he said as he came thumping in.

She looked up with a smile. "Good morning, Matthew. How do scrambled eggs sound this morning?"

"Perfect," Matt said. If he'd wanted something else, he knew she would have cheerfully provided it for him. "Hi, guys," he added, joining the two youngest members of the Ryder family at the table.

"We beat you today!" four-year-old Jenny told him triumphantly. It was a rare morning that he wasn't up before them and eating breakfast with their father. "We were here first."

"I've been up for hours," Matt told her solemnly. "This is lunch I'm having now." She looked so disappointed that he winked at her to let her know it wasn't true. "Where's your mom?"

"In her room," Michael said, adding with a heavy sigh, "She's writing."

Matt laughed. He too had discovered that when their mother became involved in the lives and misfortunes of her imaginary characters it was impossible to get her attention unless you were bleeding to death at her feet. "You don't think she's forgotten, do you?" he said to Michael.

"Forgotten what?" said a voice from the hall. Sally Ryder appeared in the doorway wearing an air of vague confusion that Matt knew at once was being put on for his benefit.

Michael, who was five-and-a-half and took life very seriously, had more trouble telling the fake from the real thing. "Don't you remember?" he said with a worried frown. "You have to take Matt to the hospital today."

"He has to get his real leg back," Jenny put in, stamping her foot in exasperation when they all began to laugh. "He does, he does!" she shouted.

An hour later, when the cast was sawn apart and fell away, Matt no longer felt like laughing. His first glimpse of the pale shrivelled limb that had barely survived three months' incarceration in plaster left him wishing he could have had it Jenny's way after all.

"Exercise it, by all means," the doctor said in answer to his anxious question. "Use it as naturally as you can, and it will shape right up. But don't overdo."

Don't overdo. He didn't ask because he knew the doctor would classify ten- to fifteen-mile training runs as over-doing. But for him using it naturally meant running, and he had less than five weeks before school started and the cross-country racing season began. Shape up or else, he

5

warned the leg silently. I'm not taking *maybe* for an answer.

Because Sally insisted she was in a mood for celebrating and in no hurry to get home, as soon as they checked out of the hospital they headed for the beach. For the first time since he had arrived in Los Angeles, Matt was free to race into the ocean and battle the waves. The tumultuous surge of the water, the screams of gulls, the wind whipping the wet hair off his face—everything matched the exuberance of his mood. Feeling reckless enough for anything, he even tried body surfing, but after enormous waves had pounded him into the sand a couple of times, he came back to Sally and the blanket laughing and out of breath. Quitting while he was ahead, he told her, and they sunbathed peacefully until he was dry.

Peaceful—the perfect word for Sally Ryder, Matt thought. Older than his own mother, Sally was unlike her in almost every way. His mom had been small and quick-tempered, with such a tremendous zest for living that for her the worst four-letter word in anyone's vocabulary was *can't*. Freely sharing feelings and ideas, she had challenged, encouraged, and even fought with him. She and Katie had been a lot alike.

But Sally was a listener. In the three months he had lived with the Ryders, she had made him feel that nothing he could tell her about himself, nothing he could do, would shock or disappoint her. Her capacity for understanding was like a well; no matter how many stones he dropped into it, the water level would rise to cover them.

She was a laugher, too. With her photographer's eye and her writer's sensitivity, she saw all kinds of things other people might miss. Most of them struck her as hilarious. As one wild escapade led them into another, this day turned out to be no exception.

Late in the afternoon they pulled up in the Ryders' drive. Matt was thinking that even with no one else knowing, as birthdays went, it had been one of the greatest. He had promised himself one final treat to top it off. "I can't wait to hit that pool," he said fervently as he opened the car door.

"Oh no, Matt," Sally said instantly. "You can't."

"I can't? Why not?" He glanced at his leg, half-expecting to find the cast still wrapped around it.

She smiled. "Didn't anyone ever tell you not to ask questions on your birthday?"

The answer was so unexpected that for a moment he could only stare at her. His mouth opened and closed several times, but no sound came out.

Sally laughed at his expression. "I don't know whether to be pleased that everyone managed to keep it a secret, or hurt that you really thought we didn't care enough to find out when it was." Leaning over, she kissed him lightly on the cheek. "Happy birthday, love. Wait here a moment while I find out whether it's safe for you to come inside."

You twit, he kidded himself, grinning incredulously at her departing back. Of course they cared. Birthdays were a major event in the Ryder family; he had found that out last month when Jenny turned four. Even his. Even though he wasn't family.

Late that night, long after he had turned out the light, Matt lay on his bed reliving the day and grinning into the darkness. They had already done so much for him—taking

7

him in when he was hurt and desperate and needed help, and letting him stay—that for a long time he had wished he could make some grand gesture to show them his appreciation. After today he knew it would be impossible. There was no way he could make any of them feel so welcome and so wanted. When the Ryders set out to celebrate someone's birthday, they really did a job.

Under Mrs. B's supervision, Michael and Jenny had spent the entire day blowing up balloons to float in the pool and hang from the lamp posts, winding red and white crepe paper around every outdoor chair and table leg, and painting an enormous poster that said HAPPY BIRTHDAY MATT in rainbow letters a foot high and was decorated with hundreds of smiling faces. They had decorated the cake too, and Michael proudly pointed out Matt's name half-hidden among the blobs and swirls of icing.

Lieutenant Ryder had left his work at Homicide early in honor of Matt's special day, and had brought his partner of seven years, Sergeant Tony Prado, home with him. This big, easy-going cop was the only one who had believed Matt was telling the truth last spring, when he was accused of killing Katie. Without Tony's support, Matt would not have made it through the first nightmare month after Katie's death.

Every time he saw Tony, Matt wanted to fall to one knee and swear life-long fealty and devotion, but Tony never gave him the chance. While he was stammering something dumb about how great it was to see him and thanks for coming, Tony had scooped him up as easily as if he had been Michael's size and carried him to the edge of the pool.

"Okay, kid," Tony had told him gruffly, the threat in his

voice spoiled by the laughter in his eyes, "you've been malingering around here long enough. I want to see some action!" On the last word, he had hurled him in.

Ryder had dived in after him and, with Tony close behind, chased him into the deep end. Cornering him under the diving board, they had ducked him unmercifully until Sally, Jenny, and Michael had come to his rescue. For a while the pool had been so full of flying bodies and wild laughter that it was all he could do to grab an occasional mouthful of air.

The riot in the pool had been followed by one of Mrs. B's fabulous feasts and crowned by his all-time favorite concoction—a fresh, homemade strawberry milkshake. So full of happiness and food by this time that he felt an explosion was imminent, he had found room for it somehow.

Matt grinned at the memory. For Mrs. B, he was thinking, he would have eaten it or died in the attempt.

Everyone else had presents, too. Jenny's was a four-star labor of love—a pen and pencil holder she had made herself by winding bright green yarn around a large orange juice can and gluing it on. He was amazed that she could have sat still long enough to finish it for him, and she was delighted with his approval. Sally had given him six of her favorite paperbacked books, and Tony had presented him with a card—a ridiculous card, heaping more praise on the sender than the recipient and inviting Matt to go sailing on Saturday. It was an invitation he had been looking forward to for a long time.

Michael gave him a poster he had picked out by himself. It was a two-by-three foot photograph of a wild stream chasing itself through the shadowy depths of a pine forest, a sudden painful reminder of Craigie, Idaho, and tomorrow's trip home to get some of his things before they auctioned off the rest of his family's belongings and sold the ranch. With Michael leaning on his knee as he unrolled the poster, asking anxiously if it was all right, he had killed the thought at once. As sensitive to other people's feelings as his mother, Michael would have been desolate if he thought Matt was unhappy with his present.

The best surprise of them all was Lieutenant Ryder's. Groping in the darkness for the table beside his bed, Matt found the smooth leather key case and unsnapped it one more time to finger the single key inside.

"Now that the cast is gone and you're going to be coming and going at all hours," Ryder had told him, "I wanted to make sure you could get back in the house again. And you'll need something to put the car key on when you get your license."

A key of his own. He hadn't realized it until now, but he had never wanted anything as much as he wanted this little piece of metal. It meant more than the freedom to come and go. Much more. You live here, Ryder was telling him. This is your home base. You belong.

Thank you, sir. Thanks, everybody! Tony and the Ryders had given him not just a birthday party today but a graduation ceremony, a great send-off celebration. All summer, hating himself for being so gutless, he had used the cast as an excuse to stay close to home. He had gone to baseball games with Tony and explored the city with the Ryders, but he had been afraid to go anywhere on his own and take the risk of running into a crowd of people who might recognize him and accuse him of Katie's murder.

The memory of another crowd was still with him, confused and fragmented, no longer distinct from the nightmares in which he relived the experience over and over again. Ugly faces twisting in hate, harsh voices accusing him, and pain—awful, racking pain. Matt felt himself break into a sweat. Rolling on his side he reached for the table to replace the key case, then changed his mind and slid it under his pillow instead. Keep it up, McKendrick, he kidded himself, and next thing you know you'll be sucking your thumb.

Tony was right. He had been malingering around here long enough. With the cast gone, it was time for action. And tomorrow he was going to get all the action he could handle. It would be rough, going back to a place where people had known him all his life—where they had looked at him with exasperation and amusement, with anger and affection and sometimes pride, but never with hate—and seeing the change in their faces, the hate showing through. At least he wasn't making the trip alone; the lieutenant would be there to back him up.

He was a big man—Lieutenant Ryder—lean and hard. Maybe because he hid his feelings under the unemotional façade of an experienced police detective, maybe because he seldom raised his voice but when he spoke, people listened—he seemed like the kind of guy you could imagine taking on a lynch mob in the old West and singlehandedly stopping them in their tracks. Fearless. Unshakable. Cold as ice. The kind of guy whose respect you'd give anything to earn. And the last person in the world you'd want to have know you were shook-up, sweaty-palmed, and scared out of your skull about something so simple as going home.

Relax, Matt told himself. Take it easy. It won't be all bad, not with Gary there too.

He was willing to risk a lot for the chance to see Gary. He and Gare had seldom spent more than a few days apart since the two of them were babies, sharing the same playpen and fighting over the rubber ducky. Matt grinned, trying to imagine Gary's wiry copper-colored hair and freckled face on a drooling infant. Impossible. Were babies born with freckles, he wondered, or did the spots come out later like measles?

Not funny, McKendrick, he told himself sharply. Never funny. It was measles that had made Katie deaf before she was born, before she had a chance to hear the lighthearted teasing note in her mom's voice or the warm rumble of their dad's laugh. Or him, her big brother, telling her she was a pesky little mosquito of a kid and he loved her. And it was because of her deafness that he had run away from Craigie with her last March after the car crash that had killed their mom and dad. Run away so she would not have to go to the institute for the deaf in Boise. Run away with her, and gotten her killed. . . .

Tomorrow was going to be rough all right. Feeling under the pillow, he curled his fist around the warm leather case. Whatever happened, he had a place to come back to. He could face anything, knowing that.

12

2

His eagerness to see Gary carried Matt a long way through the next day, but not quite far enough. The excited anticipation that made him kid around on the plane with Lieutenant Ryder and the stewardesses and point out familiar landmarks on the way north from Boise evaporated suddenly. One minute he was thinking about seeing Gary and feeling great. The next he was remembering everyone else in Craigie and choking on the pulse hammering in his throat. Even though he hadn't killed Katie himself, the way people thought at first he had, it was his fault she was dead. Everyone who had known Katie would hate him for it. Especially Gary's parents, Aunt Belle and Uncle Frank.

The two of them had been his parents' closest friends. They had been trying to do what was best for him and Katie after their parents died—he could see that now. But last spring he had felt betrayed. Night after night the angry arguments had raged in the Maitlands' kitchen until, to prove that the two of them could manage on their own, he and Katie had gone back to their own house to live.

The next day Sheriff Hensley had gotten into the act. Picking Matt up after school, he had driven him around the back roads in his official green and white car while he told Matt that fifteen-year-olds had no rights, no say about what happened to them in situations like this. Matt could accept the Maitlands' invitation to make his home with them, let them send Katie to the institute where she would be taught to cope with her deafness by people who were trained to help kids handicapped the way she was, and see her during vacations, or he could go on being stubborn and making things hard for everyone including himself. The only alternative was a county home.

There was another alternative. He and Katie had chosen it. Taking his mom's books so he could go on teaching Katie himself, as well as a few clothes and other necessities, he had run away with her. And now he was coming back. Alone. Of course they hated him. Why shouldn't they? He hated himself.

Stop the car! Turn around! I can't go back there now, I can't! Matt grabbed a lungful of air and hung onto it before the words could burst out and betray him. He had to go back if he wanted to see Gary. And if he was going to see Gary, he would have to take his chances with Gary's mom and dad. A package deal. All or nothing. Come on, McKendrick, he told himself furiously. You can't chicken out now.

Clenching one fist tightly around the other, Matt made himself concentrate on the world outside the car windows instead of the one inside his head. Phone poles, pasture fences, grazing cattle, an occasional figure on bicycle or horseback—all swept into and out of his vision as if he were watching a wide-screen movie without the sound track. Not much plot, he thought, trying to kid himself out of his panic. No Academy Awards for this production, guys.

He spoke too soon. In the sun-bleached sky ahead of them a flock of birds clustered in an agitated swarm, crows swooping and darting around a dark core of frenzied activity like a crowd of kids watching a fight. Above the engine's high-pitched hum and the wind rushing past the open window, Matt heard their shrill and savage cawing. He shivered, remembering sounds like that from his nightmares.

A small black shape suddenly burst out of the thickest part of the swarm and plummeted toward the earth. Spreading clumsy wings a few yards above the ground, it flew to refuge in a ragged oak. As the car went past, leaving tree and birds behind, Matt did not turn around to watch. He knew the plot of this one; he had seen it several times before.

The lone crow had broken a law of the flock. It might have been diseased, or a stranger trespassing on their territory, or someone's pet set free to fend for itself. It looked no different from any other crow, but somehow they knew it didn't belong. They had turned on it and were driving it out. No trial. No chance to explain or defend itself, to apologize or promise to behave differently in the future. It had made one mistake, and that was one more than it was allowed.

It had two choices now. Accept the flock's judgment and fly as far away as it could, hiding and living the lonely life of the outlawed. Or refuse to accept. Fight back, defend itself. And eventually, under the merciless beaks and claws of its own kind, die.

Get out of there, bird! Suddenly Matt wanted to race across the fields shouting insanely and waving his arms. *I'm telling you, bird, it's not worth it. Don't fight them. Get the hell out of there while you can* . . . "—and don't come back!"

"Did you say something, Matt?"

Matt glanced at the lieutenant, not realizing he had spoken out loud. Ryder was looking at him, his remote gray eyes appraising Matt thoughtfully before he turned his gaze back to the road. Reading me like a book, Matt thought. He knows I'm in a sweat, and there's no way I can hide it from him. But at least I can count on him not to ask me why.

Three months ago, when he had been a ruthless detective from Homicide and Matt a kid accused of murder, Lieutenant Ryder would have demanded an explanation and Matt—afraid of the consequences if he refused—would have given him one. Their relationship had changed completely since the night the lieutenant had decided Matt was telling the truth about Katie, but Matt would have given a lot to know whether Ryder still thought of him privately as the original gutless wonder. The last thing he wanted was to give him any more reasons to.

"No, sir, nothing important." A moment later, grateful for the diversion, he told Ryder to turn left.

"Almost there?"

"Almost." A couple of miles up the black-topped country road, he told the lieutenant to turn left again.

16

"This isn't your place," Ryder commented as they drove through the gate and rattled across the cattle guard. *F. B. Maitland* was painted on the mailbox and carved into the crossbar overhead.

"It's the Maitlands'," Matt said unnecessarily and grinned in spite of himself at the lieutenant's exaggerated look of surprise. "We can get a key to the house from them," he explained. *And find out how they feel about Katie and me . . . as if I didn't know.* Wish me luck, crow, he thought. My turn's coming.

Maneuvering himself out of the car, Matt opened the yard gate and closed it again after Ryder had driven through. He flicked a nervous glance at the barn and found his luck was in. The pickup was gone and Uncle Frank with it. Gary's Honda was missing too, but as soon as he heard Matt was back, he'd be burning rubber all the way out to the McKendrick ranch.

Matt climbed back into the car grinning. He was remembering the time Gary had roared up to their back door on his new trail bike and skidded into the porch, knocking the steps six inches off center. As Ryder drove slowly around the gravelled circle beside the two-story white house, scattering chickens and raising a last small cloud of dust, Matt's grin died. He and Gary were going to celebrate, and soon. But first he had to pay the price.

Once the engine was turned off, it was a moment or two before Matt became aware of sounds he had almost forgotten: a horse whinnying in the pasture across the creek; a bee zinging past with a self-important hum; the chickens making pleased, soft clucking sounds like old ladies talking to themselves in the supermarket as they

17

hunted and pecked their way around the yard; the thunder of the Maitland dogs barking a warning and wagging a welcome at the same time. Hedging their bets, his dad always said when they did that.

The air had its own smells, too—different from Los Angeles. A faint, sweet mixture of dust, new-mown hay, and freshly baked pie. Matt took a deep breath, soaking up the familiar atmosphere like a dried-out sponge. He could feel himself expanding, loosening up, getting his strength back as if after a long illness. He was home.

Come on, he told himself sharply. Quit stalling. Go find Aunt Belle and get it over with.

He was moving slowly toward the house when two of the dogs detached themselves from the mob and came to meet him, sniffing warily at his legs. Matt stopped suddenly, staring.

It couldn't be them. Not Poor Boy and Pat—not his own dogs. They were gone, weren't they—like everyone else? He gave a shaky laugh. "Boy . . . ? Pat . . . ? Is it really—?"

Barking wildly at the sound of his voice, they hurled themselves at him, bowling him over and covering his face with joyful, slobbery kisses. Laughing and crying, he rolled with them on the grass, thumping their woolly ribs and trying breathlessly to fend them off. "Oh you crazy dogs—you big old crazy mutts—how could I forget you?" You and the hot dusty round-ups, the early morning runs, the cold nights camping out in the hills with Gare and sharing a sleeping bag with two warm furry bodies. . . . "How could I forget you?"

18

The familiar squeak and slam of the Maitlands' kitchen door, and Gary's mom hollering across the yard, "You dogs —stop that now, you hear me?" brought the welcome to a sudden end. Disentangling himself with difficulty, Matt struggled to his feet. Aunt Belle was hurrying toward them with a broom in her hands, ready to whomp the dogs and rescue the stranger she was expecting to see from their unfriendly assault. When she saw who he was, what would she do? Use the broom on him instead? Drive him off the property and tell him never to come back? Or just look at him, recognition giving way to silent accusation and the hatred he was afraid to see before she turned her back on him and walked away? She was getting close. It was too late to get back in the car and drive away. Too late to turn around and run. He swiped at his tear-streaked face with a dusty sleeve. "Hello, Aunt Belle," he said quietly.

She was not his real aunt, but except for that one time last spring when she had sided with the sheriff and Uncle Frank, she had always treated him as if she were—hugging him when she felt like it, listening to him when he needed her to, fussing and worrying over his disasters, and bawling him out when he had it coming. More than an aunt. More like a mother. *Oh God, Aunt Belle, make it quick if you're going to—*

The broom teetered on its bristles and fell forgotten to the ground. "Matt?" she said faintly. "Matt, love, you've come back?" She searched his face as if looking for answers to questions of her own. Suddenly she found them. Almost shouting, she smothered all his doubts about her feelings for him in her strong bony arms. "Oh Matt . . . Matt,

I'm so glad you're back! I was so afraid, after everything that happened, you'd never want to see us again. Come on inside and— Oh shoot! Gary's not here. But he'll be home soon. You can wait, can't you? Oh, he'll be so glad you're back! He's missed you something terrible. We all have. Come right on in and tell me all your news. You still riding unbroke horses and climbing around on barn roofs where you don't belong?"

Swept along on the tide of her breathless conversation and the waves of relief surging through him, Matt was on the porch and almost inside the kitchen before he remembered Lieutenant Ryder. "I can't stay, Aunt Belle," he said apologetically, glancing over his shoulder at the car.

"Of course you can stay, Matt. Your friend too. You haven't driven all this way—you drove up from Boise this morning, didn't you?—not to have a cold drink. Invite your friend in, Matt. Beer . . . iced tea . . . Coke?"

"Thanks, Aunt Belle. We'd like to, but Lieutenant Ryder has to go into Craigie to see Sheriff Hensley, and we have an appointment with Dad's lawyer at three-thirty. I need to go up to the ranch and get some things before they have the auction."

For the first time in his life, he had silenced Gary's mom. Standing in the doorway, absent-mindedly holding the screen door open, she aged ten years while he was watching. He knew she was remembering his parents' funeral and all the bad times that followed it. Embarrassed by the unfamiliar twistings of grief on her normally laughing face, he looked down at Poor Boy, who was pushing his cold nose into Matt's hand. With careful concentration he scratched the dog behind its flopping ears.

"Matt." Her voice was low and sad. He couldn't look at her. "Matt, I'm so sorry, love. I wish— We never meant— Oh!" She drew a quick breath. "Matt, Poor Boy really misses you. You want to take him? I could send him down. They'd let you keep him, wouldn't they? Of course they would."

He was glad to hear her revving up again, but he wished she hadn't brought up this thing about Poor Boy. Boy had been his ever since he found the scraggly pup someone had thrown out of a car window on the road into town. For a second he was torn. Someone from home with him down there in Los Angeles? If he couldn't have Gare—

"No!" he said sharply. You don't take a ranch dog, raised to work for his keep and used to roaming free, and pen him up in your backyard in a city, no matter how much you want him. Not if you love him.

Aunt Belle reached for his free hand and squeezed it roughly. "I should have guessed you wouldn't do that to him, Matt. I know you well enough. I guess I just wanted to say—to tell you how much I— Oh shoot!" Shutting her mouth in a tight line, she got a grip on herself. "Well, don't let me keep you then, love. I know you must be anxious to get home and— But you'll be sure and come by here on your way back, won't you? Oh, and you'll need the key." Getting it for him off the nail where it had been hanging for the past seventeen years, she sent him off with one last rib-crunching hug.

He had almost reached the car when he remembered what he had really come for. "Aunt Belle," he called. "When Gary comes home, will you tell him I'm—"

"Don't you worry, Matt. I'll get right on the phone and see if I can't find him. He'll be so glad!"

She was still standing in the doorway as they drove off. Matt leaned out the window to shout one more "Thank you!" and nearly scalped himself on a passing branch. He could not believe the change in the way he felt. The knots in his chest had untied themselves; the weight on his lungs was gone. He wanted to whoop and holler and race the lieutenant's car all the way down the blacktop to his own gate and up the driveway to his own house. Anchored to the car by his feeble leg, he let his mouth do the running instead. Nonstop gibble-gabble his mom would have called it, but the lieutenant didn't seem to mind. Laughing off Matt's apology for leaving him behind, Ryder asked all kinds of questions and encouraged Matt to keep talking whenever he seemed to be running down.

When they turned in under the *MCK Ranch* sign a mile further up the blacktop, Matt unbuckled his seat belt. Leaning forward impatiently, he pointed out the duck pond where on hot summer nights they had all swum together, the corral where he had been thrown by an untrained pinto and had broken his other leg, and the tree with the triple trunk and hollow base where Pat always had her pups and where Katie used to hide when she was running away from home.

When they finally reached the house, Matt jackknifed his long frame out of the car while the lieutenant kept the engine idling. "Sure you don't want any help?" Ryder asked, giving Matt a chance to change his mind about being left alone in a house full of memories.

He had spent the last day looking forward to seeing Gary and the last hour dreading his meeting with Aunt Belle. Apart from deciding what he was going to keep, he had not given the problem of returning to his own house much thought at all. Buoyed by the exuberant welcome he had received, his mind on the coming reunion with Gare, he was not worried about the next forty-five minutes. "I guess not, thanks. I can handle it. There's not much to get, and I know where everything is."

Ryder nodded. "All right, then. I'll be back in about an hour." He drove away and left Matt standing in his yard alone.

3

With the fading hum of the rental car filling his ears, Matt did not understand at first what was wrong. The house, needing a coat of paint, looked smaller and shabbier than he remembered, and the closed windows gave it a shut-up look he was not used to; but it was still home. The weathered gray barn looked exactly the way he remembered, except that the big doors had been rolled shut and a new padlock gleamed above the crossbar. The shrubs around the house were wild and uncut, and what he could see of his mom's vegetable garden out back was a mass of weeds. There was nothing in the front yard except a pile of old ashes. Everything looked familiar, but something was missing.

Sniffing the air, he got only a trace of exhaust fumes. He listened. A white butterfly, fluttering past to light soundlessly on the yard gate, emphasized the stillness. Judging by the weeds tangled around it, the gate itself had not been shut for a long time. Nothing lived here to keep in or out. Nothing, and nobody, lived here anymore.

The contrast with the warm lively atmosphere of the Maitlands' ranch gave Matt the feeling he was looking at a movie sound stage—an empty imitation of the real thing. The outward shape of the ranch had remained intact, but the heart of it was missing. Everything important, everything that had made this place a home, was gone.

Limping up the front steps, he struggled with the stiff lock for a moment, the feeling that he was as much a stranger here as he was in Los Angeles growing stronger every second. The door swung inward, creaking. He stepped into the front hall, the unnatural silence reminding him of the abandoned cabin in the hills that he and Gary had found and explored one summer long ago. As he went slowly into the living room, dust motes swirled around him in the sunlight.

The green armchair by the fireplace still held memories of his dad's big frame—a depression in the seat cushion and a dent high on the back. He had sat in that chair many times and measured himself against that same dent to see how much farther he had to go before he was as tall as the dark-haired giant he resembled in so many other ways. They'd had a bet with each other that by his sixteenth birthday he would be the same height—six feet, six.

I didn't make it, Dad. I probably never will. I haven't grown much since you— Since you and Mom—

The house had tricked him, caught him off guard with its silence and its emptiness. He had thought he was going to be safe from memories in this dead and unfamiliar place, but months of practice conjuring up living images of Gary whenever he needed someone safe to talk to had made him too good at it. For a second he saw his father's strong weathered face, amusement and approval glinting in the dark eyes, hidden laughter making the corners of his mouth twitch. Then the image blurred. The eyes became blank and staring. The slack mouth was torn at the corner, and across one side of the face was a raw darkened patch.

"No, Dad! *No!*" The room lurched and spun, throwing him off balance. Fighting for control, he grabbed blindly for the photograph on the mantel taken at last year's rodeo —Katie on Pedro and himself on the Black, their mom and dad on Tomboy and Tripoli. Without looking at it, he fled down the hall to the bathroom, where he gulped handful after handful of water until the front of his shirt was soaking but the pain inside was drenched and dulled.

He would not go into the kitchen after all; too many of their good times had been celebrated in that room. And their bad, he thought, stopping himself before the memory could get any stronger of Katie's bright-eyed baby face peering happily over his sobbing mother's shoulder on the day they learned she was deaf.

As if to cancel out the bad one, another memory presented itself. Because he wanted something good to think about, he let it come. He had gotten home from school one afternoon to find his mom working with the three-year-old Katie, teaching her to say the sounds she could feel in her throat and see on her lips and tongue, but could not hear. Before he could come in, his mom had told him sharply to wait outside the back door. He had done as she said, jiggling restlessly from one foot to the other because as usual he had waited until he got home to go to the bathroom and listening without really hearing them to the odd, gruff little noises Katie was making. It sounded like she was saying "mad." A good word for his little sister to know, he thought with a grin. She had a temper every bit as wild as his mom's and his.

"Hey, Mom," he said impatiently through the screen door. "I have to go to the—"

"Hush up and wait!" she hissed at him, and a second later added, "—Matt."

"Can I come in now?" he said, before it hit him. That voice didn't belong to his mom!

"Matt-Matt-MATT!"

"Come on, Matt—hurry up!" his mother was yelling. "When she says it right, you have to come, so she knows!"

His mom was laughing when he burst through the door —laughing and crying—and Katie was squealing delightedly and clapping her hands as if she thought she had magicked him up out of nowhere by saying his name, and he had hugged his baby sister and his mom and his baby sister again and gone flying out of the door and away down the road, the dogs leaping and barking around him, shouting for his father so he could share the great news. *Katie said my name, Dad! Katie said my—*

Matt cut off the memory abruptly. He had come here to do a job. If he didn't get moving, it wouldn't get done. Dumping the linens and blankets from his dad's battered army foot locker onto his parents' bed and carrying the small trunk into the living room, he set it down in front of the bookshelves and began filling it with books, relieved to discover that by concentrating on finding the ones he

27

wanted he could keep his mind safely in the present and away from the past.

Finished with the books, he retrieved a couple of suitcases from the storeroom and carried them upstairs. He was looking forward to packing his own things, but he went into Katie's room first, finding what he was looking for under her bed. It was a cardboard file-folder crammed with sketches, half-finished stories and photographs. He picked one snapshot out at random and found himself looking at the blurred face of a bewildered coon peering out of the cage behind the barn where Katie kept and doctored all the hurt animals she found until they were well enough to set loose again.

The next picture he remembered Katie taking. It was Gary, grinning proudly on his new Honda. In the background was Matt himself, scowling and gesturing in mock rage at the damage to the porch steps. Laughing, Matt sent his good buddy an urgent message. *Come on, Gare—hurry up! You're wasting valuable time.*

Stuffing everything back in the folder and snapping the heavy rubber band around it, Matt took it and the two suitcases across the narrow hall into his own room. Opening the suitcases out on the bed, he looked up at the wall facing him. He was expecting to see the team pictures, the newspaper clippings, the photographs and certificates starting with his first winning run at the age of nine that recorded most of his off-ranch life right up to the last basketball game they had played against Grant Consolidated the week before his parents died.

The utter blankness of the wall, dotted with tag ends of

transparent tape and blotched with the sun-printed outlines of rectangles and squares, bewildered and stunned him. He gazed blankly around the dusty little room, half-expecting to find he was in someone else's house. The rolltop desk, the oak bureau, and the homemade bookshelves were his, but someone had swept them clean of all his tropies, too.

Who would have taken them . . . a burglar? The silver ones, maybe, but most of his trophies were brass or plastic, and the one Katie had made for him in kindergarten one Christmas was a shapeless, rainbow-colored lump of clay.

Who even knew about them, besides Gary? Gary . . . ? That made even less sense, but there was a sure way to tell. Matt flung open his closet door. Gary was the only one who knew about his box safe. If it was gone. . . . Sweeping aside the pile of magazines on the top shelf, he saw the scarred wooden box in the corner. Relief washed over him. Not Gary.

Who then? Matt lifted the box down. Without opening it he had his answer. It was too light. Even before he shook it, he knew it was empty.

For one long uncomprehending moment he held the box in front of him, staring into its dull finish as if he could see what had happened to the track medals, the ribbons, the team letters, the pill bottle with the tiny flakes of gold that he and Gary had laboriously panned out of Little Creek last summer—all the odds and ends of his life that meant something special, that said something about who he was and where he had been.

He needed those souvenirs of his past. He had counted

on taking them back to L.A. so he would not feel completely cut off from the first sixteen years of his life; so he would have a link with the one place in the world where people really knew him and knew he was okay. He could understand Gary taking a couple of things to remember him by, but not everything. It was crazy. Something was wrong.

Suddenly, he realized that the distant buzz he'd been hearing was not someone's chain saw. Gary's Honda was coming up the drive flat out, a desperate urgency in the straining sound of the engine. *Too late, Maitland old buddy, I already know.* But why? He could think of several answers to that question, and there was only one he could live with. If it wasn't that one. . . .

Ignoring his weak leg, Matt took the stairs three at a time and burst out the front door as Gary was hanging his black and yellow helmet on the handlebars. The door slammed behind him, and Gary glanced up, a grin spreading rapidly across his freckled face. "Hey, man, it's great to see you! When Mom told me—"

Matt had to get the question answered fast. Everything depended on Gary's answer. "What did you do with my stuff?"

Gary's grin vanished abruptly. "H . . . how did you know?"

Matt felt he was rushing headlong into disaster, but he couldn't stop. "How did I know? How do you think I knew? You're the only one I ever told about the box in the closet—that's how I knew. What did you do with my stuff?"

Gary's gaze shifted guiltily. Matt turned to see what he was looking at. The ring of old ashes. While he was figuring it out, Gary tried to head him off. "Matt, wait a second. I have to—"

"You burned it?" This couldn't be happening. It had to be a stinking nightmare. "You burned it all—everything?" He took a threatening step toward Gary. "What about the stuff that wouldn't burn?"

Gary swallowed, his freckles like splattered paint on his white face. "Threw it in Big Creek. Matt, listen—"

"Threw it in—!" Matt was past listening. He swung on Gary, knocking him backwards into his bike. "You creep—I needed that stuff! Why did you do it?"

Extricating himself from the bike, Gary gave the place where his leg and the hot exhaust pipe had connected a quick rub. His scarlet ears gave away his rising anger, but he set his bike up again with elaborate care before he answered Matt. "Because," he said through clenched teeth, "I thought the Matt McKendrick I knew was either dead or never existed."

Dead . . . ?

Dead. *Oh God . . . I wish I were.* "You believed them?" *Not you, good buddy. Anyone else—I can take it from anyone else. But not you.* "You believed Sheriff Hensley?" His voice rose uncontrollably. "But you knew me, Gare—me and Katie. You knew I could never—"

"Nobody gave me any choice, Matt," Gary broke in, his own voice high and thin. "It was just the sheriff saying Katie was dead and you killed her. How was I supposed to know?"

31

Katie is dead. You killed her. It was not the first time Matt had heard those words. But getting them from strangers was one thing. Getting them from Gary was another. "You should have known!" he cried, the agony so real and rough-edged he thought he was being torn apart. "I loved her. I never could have hurt her. You knew that—and you believed them!"

"Matt, listen," Gary pleaded desperately. "I'm sorry."

"Forget you, creep! I don't need your apologies. I don't need you either. I had this crazy idea I had a friend up here, but I was—"

"Listen to me, you jerk!" Gary screamed. "Listen to me! You think you were the only one who went through hell? You ever wonder what it's like having the whole world tell you your best friend's murdered his own sis—?"

"Don't say it, you—!"

"You know what I went through, knowing it was me who helped you run away? You know how I felt when I heard about Katie? If I'd kept my mouth shut, she might be in an institution, but she'd still be alive, and I—"

Matt hurled himself at Gary. They went down together in a tangle of flailing fists and thrashing legs, raging incoherently and spattering each other with bitter, furious tears. All at once Gary tore himself out of Matt's grip and was up and running for his bike.

"Go to hell, McKendrick, you creep!" he screamed over the howling engine. "Maybe they're right! Maybe you are crazy enough to kill someone accidentally—only I'm not crazy enough to hang around and find out!"

Matt stumbled to his feet, but the bike shot off down

the drive, spraying him with pebbles and dirt. "Go to hell yourself, Maitland!" he screamed after it. "You're the one who's crazy—not me!" Picking up a rock, he hurled it as far down the road as he could and ran for the house.

Back in his room a moment later, he flung his clothes and other unimportant things into the suitcases, swearing all the wildest and worst words he knew while tears he couldn't stop made spots and splotches everywhere they fell. Dumping both cases in the front hall, he made a couple of trips upstairs for his books and was slamming the footlocker on the last load when he heard the crunch of tires on the gravel turnaround. Ryder was back. Great! He couldn't wait to get away from this house—away from this whole lousy town. All he had to do was get through the next couple of hours somehow and he'd be on his way back to L.A. for good.

What did I tell you, bird? he said bitterly to the outlawed crow. Get the hell out and don't come back. I should have taken my own advice.

Getting through the hours that followed proved hard to do. Somewhere between his own house and the lawyer's office, his rage died suddenly, leaving him alone with the pain. He made himself go through the motions with Mr. Brice, trying to listen and say the right things, but none of it seemed important anymore. On the long trip home he was silent and withdrawn, and Ryder used the time on the plane to catch up on some paperwork he had brought along. By the time they were letting themselves into the big white house in the L.A. hills, Sally was the only one still up and waiting to hear how it had gone.

33

"Okay, I guess," Matt said in answer to her question. "I got everything I wanted."

He was counting on her to understand that he didn't want to talk about it, and she didn't let him down. Exchanging a glance with her husband, she carried one of his suitcases down to his room, while filling him in on Jenny's latest escapade, and kissed him good night. Pausing on her way out, she said gently, "It was rough, wasn't it? Worse than you expected. I'm sorry, love," and was gone before he had to think of a reply.

It's okay, he told her silently, shedding his clothes and falling heavily into bed. As long as I still have all of you, it's okay. It was his last coherent thought before he plunged into exhausted sleep.

4

One instant he was dreaming. The next he was awake—
sweating and trembling, his harsh breathing the only sound
in the dark room. The nightmare again. The same one,
only this time—

"Matt?" A tall figure was silhouetted in the dim rectangle
of his open door. "You awake?"

Oh lord . . . he must have been yelling if he had woken
up the lieutenant. How many times did this make? Five.
And he wasn't a little kid anymore; he should have out-
grown nightmares long ago. Matt swallowed, grateful for
the darkness that hid his tearstained face. "Yes, sir, I'm
awake."

"Want to talk?"

Talking helped, but they had said it all before, and there
was no point in going over the same ground. What he did
want was to tell Ryder he was sorry he was such a snivel-
ling coward, but he couldn't even do that; a couple of
nightmares ago the lieutenant had made him promise not
to apologize anymore. The sooner he learned to handle

this, the better it would be for both of them. "No, I'm okay now. Thanks."

Ryder remained in the doorway, motionless. It seemed a long time before he spoke again. "Matt. . . ."

Don't ask, Matt begged him silently. Jesus . . . please don't ask. I'll break down and tell you everything, and you'll know for certain what a gutless wonder I—

"All right, Matt," Ryder said quietly, as if he had heard Matt's silent plea, "if you're sure."

"I'm sure. It was the same as all the others."

"The crowd attacking you?"

"Yes."

"Nothing else? Nothing new?"

"No." *Yes, but I can't tell you about that either.*

"All right," he said again. "Good night, then. You know what to do."

"Yes." Turn on the light and read for a while so he wouldn't find himself back in the same dream when he went to sleep. But that wasn't what he was afraid of this time. "Good night, sir. And thanks."

Instead of turning on the light after Ryder left, Matt flipped the soggy pillow onto its dry side and lay back, hands under his head, staring into the darkness. It had been the same nightmare; he had not lied about that. Up to a point it had been the same lousy dream. Himself alone in a strange city, searching for Katie, racing desperately down dark streets, calling her name. Suddenly rounding a corner and running into a crowd of ordinary people. Blurting out a plea for help.

Their faces changing—seeing a guy who killed a little

girl and got away with it. Hating him. Eyes hard and ugly, mouths screaming accusations. *You killed her! You shouldn't be walking around free and clear; you should be punished for what you did!*

Trying to run. Caught. Thrown to the ground yelling *No, no—I didn't do it!* Held down. Begging them to listen.

But they don't. They're all over me—kicking, hitting, screaming that I've got to pay for hurting her. Sometimes . . . oh God . . . sometimes they have knives—

Matt sat bolt upright. Panting hoarsely, he fumbled for the light switch. Jesus! He couldn't even think about it when he was awake without coming apart. Maybe if he got up and splashed cold water on his face, walked around a little. . . .

Fifteen minutes later he was back in bed, debating whether to leave the light on and deciding against it. On the wall at the foot of his bed was Michael's birthday poster. Looking at it would only make things worse. He had to forget Craigie and everyone in it. Especially Gare.

Gare. That was the thing that made this nightmare different from the others. And worse. Gare in the crowd, hating him, screaming at him like everyone else.

No wonder he had gone crazy this afternoon. No wonder he felt so shaky and uncertain now. The one person who knew him better than anyone else in the world—who knew everything there was to know about him, the good and the bad—believed he was capable of hurting someone he loved as much as Katie.

He had counted on Gare. Without him there was no

one left who had always known him and who could swear he was okay. Gare had been his secret weapon, his trump card, his proof that he wasn't the kind of guy that everyone who knew only what they'd read in the papers about him thought he was.

He hadn't expected life in L.A. to be easy. Even if nine out of every ten people who read about him last spring had forgotten him by now, he was going to run into the tenth one, the one who remembered the story and the photographs, again and again. There was no way he could avoid it, and no way to tell in advance when it was going to happen. Every time he stuck his neck outside the Ryders' door, or got on a bus, or walked into a classroom, he was going to have to be ready for someone to say, *Hey, aren't you the guy who killed a little girl and got away with it?* And once one person knew, it wouldn't take long for the word to get around.

What kind of guy was he? That was the question people would be asking themselves once they knew the story. If they didn't actually accuse him of the murder, they'd be looking at him with a question in their eyes, giving him a wide berth.

You can take that kind of stuff from strangers as long as you know something they don't know. That they're wrong—dead wrong. That you aren't the kind of guy they think you are. But what happens when you aren't sure what kind of guy you are anymore? When your best friend, who's known you since Day One, says he was wrong about you, how can you be sure that you're right?

Face it, McKendrick. You aren't the same guy you were

before all this happened. That guy had so many people in his life who knew he was okay he didn't have to worry about what the rest of the world thought. He could damn the torpedoes and plow straight ahead. But you—! You're scared to set foot outside the house. You don't even want to get your toes wet anymore.

If you know so much—what kind of guy am I?

You really want me to tell you?

Yes. No . . . forget I asked.

You're a guy who made a mistake you're never going to stop paying for. A guy wearing a label a mile high that tells every new person you meet that you're dangerous, you can't be trusted, it's not safe to have you around. A guy who's going to spend the rest of his life like that crow—alone. You better start getting used to the idea.

I won't buy that. People can change their minds.

They can, but what makes you think they will? If Gary could believe that story, how are you going to convince all the strangers you're going to be running into from now on that it isn't true?

I convinced Tony, didn't I? And the Ryders.

How?

I don't know.

Gary changed his mind about you, and he knew you better than they ever will.

Don't say it.

The lieutenant and Sally don't know you very well.

Don't say it, you jerk!

Something could happen, like it did with Gare. They could change their minds about you too.

You're crazy! Lieutenant Ryder . . . maybe. But not Sally and Tony.

That's what you thought about Gare.

Oh Jesus . . . I can't lose them too. Not them.

Oh yes you can. That's another idea you'd better start getting used to. . . .

5

Matt overslept the next morning, finding Michael chatting with Mrs. B in the kitchen when he came in. Last night he had been ready to spend the rest of his life in his locked bedroom, but then his uncompromising inner voice had given him a positive idea to wrestle with.

There was nothing he could do to change people's minds about him. People were going to think what they liked, and there was no way he could prove they were wrong. But he had one thing going for him still, one part of him that hadn't changed. He was a runner, and a good one. It was something he *could* prove to the world—something small, but all he had left on the plus side. He would make people recognize it and add it to their one-sided view of him if it killed him.

Having the running to concentrate on would make it easier to live with the rest of his problems, but the leg needed a lot of work. If he was going to build it up in time for the cross-country, he had to get started.

"I'm going to take a hike up that side road at the top

of the hill, Michael," he said as he finished breakfast. "I want to see if it's a good area for running. Want to come?"

His nightmare was so vivid in his mind that the instant the words were out he wanted to take them back. Make Michael stay at home, safe. But how could he make Michael understand? Tell him there might be trouble and he didn't want him there? What kind of trouble? Michael would ask. Why don't you want me? Questions he couldn't answer. If he saw trouble coming, he would just have to grab Michael and run like hell.

A few minutes later they were walking up Verde Canyon Road and turning left on the narrow side street named Las Lomas. Birds called from tree to tree, and small creatures rustled furtively in the shrubbery as they walked by. Trouble seemed unlikely in this remote and peaceful setting. Reminded of other early morning runs, Matt was suddenly impatient to get started. "Come on, Michael. Let's jog for a little ways."

"What's jog?"

"A slow run, like this." He demonstrated, and Michael trotted happily along beside him for a while before he began to drop back. Matt did not want to let him get too far behind, but he was anxious to test his leg and his wind. "I'll stop and wait for you at that big tree at the corner, Michael. Okay?"

Using Michael's cheerful "Okay" as a starting signal, he took off, concentrating on the weak leg. It was worse than he'd hoped, but his breathing was still good. Not too bad, he was congratulating himself as he pulled up. Not hopeless, anyway.

Oh lord. He stopped abruptly. Trouble after all, but not a kind he was expecting. Not a kind he was ready for. On the road ahead a German shepherd had come out of nowhere and was stalking him, its fangs bared. The threat of attack rattled viciously in its throat.

Taking two cautious steps backwards, he stumbled over Michael running to catch up. Matt reached behind him. "Quick, Michael, give me your hand!" A trembling hand slid into his, and he hoisted the small boy up on his back. "If he tries to bite you," he said in a low voice, "kick him as hard as you can."

"What if he bites you?" Michael quavered in his ear.

Against his back he could feel the terrified beating of the little boy's heart. "Let him try!" he said savagely. Before he'd let the monster hurt Michael, he would kill it. Worry about its owners later. If he *could* kill it. . . . "Hey!" he yelled. "Hey, help us somebody! We need help!"

The dog crouched. It was going to spring.

You bastard, Matt thought in silent fury. Come on, then —what are you waiting for? Michael's whispered "Someone's coming" took a moment to sink in.

Someone coming? Let it be someone old enough to help, Matt prayed. "Hey," he shouted, "can you help us get this monster off?"

Fifteen feet away the someone stopped. Risking a quick glance, Matt saw a guy about his own age. "That damned dog!" the guy yelled. "So far he's been all bluff and no bite, but he's really going to attack someone someday." Someday soon, Matt thought. "Hey Boo, you mutt . . . beat it!" The guy shagged a couple of rocks at the dog's flanks.

"Go on, Boo, get home! Get out of here, you stupid mutt!"

Boo slunk snarling into the bushes. With a trembling Michael still clinging to his back, Matt moved cautiously away from the dog's territory. Now that the danger from the animal was over, he realized he was in as big a sweat about the stranger he was going to have to meet as he had been about the dog.

Come on, McKendrick, he told himself scornfully. You'll know in the first couple of seconds if he's one of the nine who doesn't know you, or the tenth guy who does. Just tell him thanks for saving your lives, and then if you have to, you can run like hell for the Ryders'.

The vision of himself fleeing in terror from their astonished rescuer with Michael bouncing wildly on his back made Matt grin in spite of himself. He took a deep breath and kept on walking.

"Thanks," he said as soon as he was within range. "You've got a great throwing arm. Play much baseball?" He was counting the seconds, watching the boy's eyes for a change of expression.

"Tennis," said their rescuer with a grin. He flipped his last two rocks in the ditch. "Glad I could help."

One of the nine. Matt realized he had been holding his breath, and let it out slowly and gently. "So am I."

The guy was wearing cutoffs split up the side, a sweat band around his thick sun-bleached hair, and old tennis shoes. Not a serious runner, Matt decided as he took this in, but he probably knew the neighborhood. "Where do you do your running?" he asked. "I was going to map out a course to run myself until that monster got in the way."

The boy turned, pointing back the way he had come. "Well, if you go around that corner, there's a— Wait a second, I'll take you up to the Loop. It's easier to describe it from there."

Walking up the road with him, Matt wondered how old the guy was. His voice was deep, but he was about five inches shorter than Matt and, except for a pair of wide shoulders, kind of lean and stringy for his height. His face was thin and square-jawed, and his brown eyes glinted mischievously as he asked, "Do you always run with a load like that?"

Matt grinned. "Only the first twenty miles," he said, adding over his shoulder, "Let me know, Michael, when you want to get down, okay?" Hitching the small boy higher on his back, he gave Michael's legs a reassuring squeeze to tell him there was no hurry.

"Are you new around here?" the boy asked.

"Not here. We live on Verde Canyon."

"The white house with the red tile roof," Michael put in. "I can get down now, Matt."

"That's our house." The guy was pointing at a sand-colored, stucco ranch-style on the downhill side of the street. "I'm Will," he added when he saw Matt looking at the *T. J. Schuyler* on the mailbox.

"I'm Matt—" he began automatically, but sheer funk jammed in his throat and strangled the *McKendrick* before he could get it out. "And this is Michael," he went on rapidly, hoping Will hadn't noticed anything odd and calling himself every kind of coward he could name.

But he didn't have to go around advertising himself to

everyone he met, did he? The only people who had to know were the ones who were going to be seeing a lot of him, and he might never see this guy again. "Do you run at school?" he asked, to get the conversation back to safer ground.

"No, I jog because it keeps me in shape for tennis and skiing. Do you?"

"I'm planning on it," Matt said grimly. "If I can shape up this leg in time."

Will eyed the offending limb critically. "It does look a shade off-color. What have you been doing to it? Testing different brands of suntan lotion for a TV commercial or something?"

Matt laughed, feeling lightheaded. After all the nights he'd spent worrying, imagining the worst, here he was kidding around with another guy as if he were an ordinary human being again. "It's been goofing off all summer in a cast."

They reached the Loop, where the road forked right and left as well as continuing straight ahead. Using a stick to draw a map in the dirt, Will described the set-up as a figure eight with Las Lomas running straight up the middle, making a course on which Matt could keep close track of times and distances.

"Sounds good," Matt said finally. "Any hills?"

"Right where the next Loop comes in," Will assured him. "A real killer. Down and up. People have been known to collapse at the bottom and have to be rescued by helicopter."

Snorting appreciatively at this description, Matt gazed longingly up the road.

"You going to try it now?" Will asked.

"No."

"I can do it, Matt," Michael put in anxiously, as if he thought it was his fault Matt couldn't go.

"I can't," Matt said. To head off further debate, he started back. Will walked them down past Boo's house, but the dog was no longer in front.

"What a stupid name for a dog like that!" Matt said, remembering what a near thing it had been for him and Michael.

"He wasn't always that bad," Will said. "When they got him, he was a friendly little fuzz-ball. He used to pop out at people and give one short bark. That's where the name came from."

"How did he get like this, then?"

"I don't know. It was after they sent him somewhere to be trained to protect their kids. Probably got to thinking he was Super Watchdog and extended his territory out farther and farther until it covered the street."

"Is there any other way to get onto Las Lomas without going past his house?"

"Not unless you run all the way to the bottom of Verde Canyon, along Montgomery Boulevard, and up the next canyon road."

"Well, I'm not going through that every day," Matt vowed. "I'll complain to his owners if he does it again— and I live through it," he added, only half-joking.

"Complaining won't do any good. I've tried. The Kennetts will tell you he's as sweet and gentle as their little old granny and put him in the backyard with their kids.

The next day he'll dig a new hole and be out on the street again."

"Oh lord!" Matt had already fought and lost several encounters with that stubborn, I've-made-up-my-mind, don't-confuse-me-with-the-facts attitude. "Well, anyway, thanks a lot. Glad you were out this morning."

"Yeah, me too." Will left them and was halfway home before he stopped and turned around. "Hey, Matt? If you want a tour guide—you know, to introduce you to the neighborhood dogs and all that—I usually run around seven when it's still cool. Just stop by and knock on the door." He paused, as if sensing Matt's sudden withdrawal, and added awkwardly, "If you want to."

Matt hesitated. Did he want this? Was Will's company for a few days going to be worth the painful confrontation over who he was that would inevitably bring it to an end? What should he tell him, yes or no? Will turned away, heading home. In a second it would be too late to tell him anything.

Take a chance, McKendrick, go on. At least you'll know it's coming. It won't hurt as much the second time around. "Okay," Matt yelled before he lost his nerve. "Thanks. If I don't make it the first couple of days, don't be too surprised. I've been sleeping in for so long, I'm all out of practice." They saluted each other, and Matt and Michael jogged to the end of Las Lomas before walking the rest of the way home.

That night, instead of eating supper with Mrs. B and the children the way he usually did, Matt had dinner late with Sally and Ryder so he could ask the lieutenant whether there was anything he could do about a dangerous dog before it hurt someone—not after when it would be too late. Describing the incident on Las Lomas, he told them he thought the dog's protective instincts were so strong it was almost insane.

Ryder considered the problem. "I don't know," he said finally. "I'll find out for you, but I have a feeling that if the dog hasn't actually done anything, about all you can do is talk to its owner. You can't get the Animal Control people out here on your hunch that something might happen someday, however educated that hunch might be."

"But, sir, a dog that size could kill someone."

"I'll ask around Headquarters tomorrow, Matt. All right?"

Matt recognized his tone. For Ryder, not a waster of words, everything that could be decided for now had been decided. There was no point in discussing it further.

Dinner over, he left the table wishing there was another way for him to get onto Las Lomas without passing the Kennetts' house so he could forget about Boo. But even if there had been ten different ways to avoid the dog, he could not turn his back on the situation now. The dog was a danger not only to him, but to everyone else on Las Lomas.

6

Boo was nowhere to be seen as Matt jogged silently past the Kennetts' house shortly before seven the next morning. Having armed himself with a handful of rocks on the way up and primed himself to fight off the slavering monster, Matt felt slightly let down. He left the rocks beside the road, where they would be available on the way home, and stopped at the top of the Schuylers' steps, suddenly afraid.

What if Will had already found out who he was? What if he came to the door and said, "Who are you trying to kid, McKendrick? Get lost!" What if he didn't come out at all—just let Matt wait out here until he got the message?

Knock it off, McKendrick, he told himself fiercely. When it happens, it happens. Until then, forget it. Or else go back to the Ryders' and spend the rest of your life under the bed. . . .

He was starting slowly down the steps when the front door opened. Will appeared, dressed in the same outfit he had worn yesterday, except for the shoes—a well-worn pair of Apollos.

"Thought you weren't serious about running," Matt said, eyeing the shoes with respect. He would have liked to own a pair himself.

"I'm not serious, not the way you are. I ran some cross-country and two-mile events in junior high, but I'm planning on going out for tennis in high school. You ready?"

"Ready as I'll ever be." Which wasn't, Matt discovered a few minutes later, saying much. His leg lasted less than one measly mile before it began to complain. He was tempted to tell it to go take a flying jump, but the doctor's warning was too fresh. He pulled up, and Will stopped with him.

"You don't have to quit," Matt said roughly, trying to hide his disappointment.

"Doesn't matter," Will said. "We can walk it for a while. I'm tour-guiding today, remember?"

Matt was pretty sure he couldn't walk more than a couple of miles on the thing either. "It's no good," he said bleakly. "I can't use it that much yet."

Will looked indecisively up the road. "Hey!" he exclaimed suddenly. "I've got a great idea—bikes! Yes, it's perfect," he insisted when Matt shook his head. "Give the leg a little exercise and then a little rest. Cover a lot of territory. See the world without pain and suffering. Schuyler Tours!" he finished with a flourish. "We get you there and back again!"

Matt grinned. Put that way it was hard to refuse. His leg was feeling better now, less like warmed-over spaghetti. He might as well give it a try.

Twenty minutes later they passed the same spot, Matt on Mr. Schuyler's ten-speed and Will on his own. Will was right. The bicycling did work better. Without the pounding on the pavement the leg was under less strain, and whenever the muscles started to heat up, he could coast and rest them for a while.

Hunched over, eyes streaming from the wind, they took the long downhill like French racers, their momentum carrying them three-fourths of the way up the other side. Will made it to the top, but Matt had to get off and push his bike the last fifteen feet. After a breathless discussion they decided to keep going straight on Las Lomas until they reached the stables.

Matt had not ridden a horse in months. Leaning on the split-rail fence, gazing downhill at the immense aluminum barn with its paddocks outside every stall, he thought longingly of the Black and wondered who had bought him at the auction. "Do they rent horses?" he said suddenly.

"I don't know. I can ask Meg. She's the horse freak in our family."

"Meg?"

"My sister. That's her horse in the third paddock."

It was a dark dapple gray, about fifteen hands. Probably part Arabian. "Nice," Matt said.

"You a horse freak, too?"

"Not—no." He had ridden horses the way most people ride bikes—mostly from necessity and sometimes for fun. Like running, though, it was something from his past that he might be able to keep alive.

"I've been on that horse exactly once," Will was saying with a grimace. "I can stay on fine in a western saddle, but Meg rides English. By the fourth bounce there wasn't any horse under me anymore."

Matt laughed. "I know that feeling." He had been bucked off more times than he could count.

"We're about two miles from our end of Las Lomas here," Will said, turning his bike around for the return trip. "If you add the loops, you can make up a ten- to fifteen-mile run when you're ready for it."

"Good," Matt said, but as he pushed his leg to its meager limits on the way back, he began to think he'd be lucky if he were ready for the short course running in the spring.

They put the bikes away and stood for a moment on the front walk, making plans to meet again.

"Tomorrow's Saturday, isn't it?" Matt said. That was his sailing day with Tony. "I think I'm up and out with the dawn's early light."

"I can't make it Sunday, either," Will said. "We've got some kind of family outing in the works."

"What about Monday then?"

"Monday's okay. You want to run or ride?"

"I don't—" Matt began, and stopped in mid-sentence. A skinny little boy, all bony knees and elbows and about eight years old, had come tearing out of the house. Laughing wildly, he slammed the front door behind him, but it flew open again. A tennis ball was hurled after him, missing Will by a hair; a girl's voice shrieked, "—and don't come back, you pig!"; and the door banged shut once more with a crash that loosened a few dead leaves from the bougainvillea climbing the wall beside it. Matt watched them floating slowly to the ground, forgetting what he had been saying as he remembered the many times he had left his own house in that wild headlong way.

"Don't mind them," Will said calmly. "Lew and Carey. One of the occupational hazards of visiting the Schuylers' gracious residence."

The small boy had taken refuge behind Will. "Hazard, schmazard," he said in a gruff voice. Retiring a safe distance first, he beaned Will neatly on the back of the head with the tennis ball and vanished, chortling, behind the garage.

"Anyway," Will said, absently rubbing his head. "Where were we?"

Matt thought back. "Monday—oh, ride or run? I was going to say I don't have a bike."

"You can use Dad's. I'll ask him, but I know he won't mind. He never uses it."

"Well . . . okay, then. Thanks. Monday at seven?"

Will acknowledged the question with a nod and a wave. Matt went off down Las Lomas, thinking about the morning behind him and the ones ahead and hoping his luck was going to hold for a while. He had completely forgotten Boo.

The dog shot out of its opened front door and rocketed up the Kennetts' steps. The pile of rocks was out of reach, and the dog meant business this time. If Boo's owner, a stocky woman with her hair in curlers, had not come out of the side yard at that moment, Matt would have been fighting for his life.

As she dragged the snarling, struggling dog down her steps and through the gate into the side yard, Matt—frightened and furious—yelled after her, "Your dog's crazy, you know that?"

"He's not crazy," she shouted, slamming the gate shut as Boo flung himself heavily against it. "He's just doing his job."

"Is keeping people from walking past your house on the street part of his job too?"

She put her hands on her hips and surveyed him. "Look, kid, don't give me a hard time about Boo. If you're scared of big dogs, maybe you should ask your mama to take you for your walk next time."

Breathing hard, Matt said a few choice words about idiot women to himself. He was about to let it go when a terrifying vision of Lew Schuyler or Michael trying to fight off the crazed and powerful dog made him try to make her see it too. "Listen, Mrs. Kennett, there are kids on this street. When Boo goes crazy enough to attack one of them, what are you going to tell his mother? That Boo was just doing his job?"

She stared at him in disbelief. He could almost see her temperature beginning to rise. "What's your name, kid?" she demanded. "I haven't seen you around here before. What are you doing here anyway?"

What's your name, kid? If she had pulled out a gun and shot him, she could not have silenced him more effectively. Matt swallowed. *Come on, McKendrick, say something and get the hell out of here before she sics her crazy dog on you.* He had only one thing left to say anyway, and he had gone too far to quit now. "I live on Verde Canyon, number twenty twenty, and I guess you ought to know that I'm going to report your dog to Animal Control."

"Your parents are going to hear from us, smart mouth.

Walking around like you owned the place. When my husband gets home . . . !"

She was still shouting as he turned onto Verde Canyon and, out of her sight, broke into a run. What are you—crazy or something? he kept asking himself incredulously. You're supposed to be keeping a low profile. Low, nothing —you're aiming at total invisibility for as long as possible. So what do you do? You get into a fight with a woman over her idiot dog, and then you tell her where you live so she can sic her husband on you when he gets home. Terrific!

He was heading up the drive when the sight of the Ryders' house stopped him cold. What had he done? He had made trouble all right, not only for himself but for the Ryders, too. The last thing he wanted to do. They wouldn't like his getting into difficulties with the neighbors. They probably didn't want the neighbors knowing who they had living with them any more than he did.

Jesus! He wished he could turn time back, start again—maybe even let Boo chew on him a little—but keep his big mouth shut.

7

On and off for the rest of the day, Matt argued with himself, eventually deciding not to say anything about Boo's owners when Lieutenant Ryder came home that night. If the Kennetts did turn up, he would deal with the problem then; if they didn't, he wouldn't have to bring Ryder into it at all.

He was dreaming if he thought they weren't coming. The lieutenant was sitting down to dinner with Sally when Boo's owners rang the doorbell. Leaving them standing on the doorstep, Ryder came down to Matt's room to get him.

"What the devil is this, Matt? Something about a dog, and you insulted the woman this morning?"

"That's not it exactly, sir, but it's my fault they're here. I'm really sorry."

It was all he had time to say before they were at the front door. Ryder opened it again and the woman said shrilly, "That's him! That's the kid who smart-mouthed me in my own front yard."

Her husband thrust himself forward. "What the hell was

all that bull about the dog? Where do you get off, coming around where you don't belong and giving my wife a hard time?"

"Just a moment," Ryder said in a tone Matt recognized with a chill. He was glad to see the couple on the doorstep were silenced by it too. "I'd like Matt to tell me what he was doing in your yard."

Matt cleared his throat. "I wasn't in the yard, sir. Just on the street. It's the dog I told you about yesterday."

"What is this thing you got against Boo?" the woman demanded.

Ryder ignored the question. "Go on, Matt," he said.

"I was walking down Las Lomas from the Schuylers' and the dog threatened me on the street again, like yesterday. If she hadn't come out when I yelled and dragged the dog off, I think it would have attacked—"

"You think?" the man interrupted angrily. "Look, mister, we've lived on that street for three years and we never had any complaints about Boo until your kid comes along."

That was a lie; Will had complained at least once. Matt opened his mouth to object, but Ryder's hand came down on his shoulder, warning him to keep quiet. When it stayed there, he felt as if the sides had suddenly evened up. Two against two.

The woman spoke up again. "I'll bet you've been throwing rocks at Boo. I'll bet that's why he doesn't like you." Something in Matt's face as he thought of the ammunition stacked in a neat pile across the street from Boo's house must have given him away. "There, you see!" she ex-

58

claimed triumphantly. "I knew it! Just look at his face. Your crummy kid comes around tormenting a poor dumb animal and making threats about calling the pound. I'll have the SPCA on you if you give us any more trouble."

"Thank you," Ryder said coldly. "I'll take care of this. Good night."

"Sir—" Matt began as the door closed.

"Save it for after dinner, Matt." Leaving him standing in the hall, Ryder went back to his interrupted meal.

In a cold sweat about the coming discussion, Matt went slowly down to his room. The interminable wait for the lieutenant to come talk to him was much worse than the anxious hours he had spent wondering whether Boo's owners were going to call, but at last Ryder came in and sat down on his bed.

"All right, Matt," he said without preamble. "Let's have the whole story."

"There isn't that much left to tell. It's like I told you yesterday, the dog is crazy. I had rocks ready this morning, but I didn't need them on the way up. It was coming back I needed them, only then they were out of reach. Sir," Matt said desperately, "I know dogs. I'm positive that one was going to try to tear me apart. I was scared. And then I got mad when she wouldn't listen, that's all."

"You didn't go into her yard?"

"No."

"Or call her rude names?"

"No." Matt grinned tentatively. "Not out loud, anyway."

Ryder snorted. "What about the threats?"

"I didn't threaten her. I said I was going to tell the Animal Control people about the dog, and I thought she should know, that's all."

"Matt," Ryder said wearily, "I don't understand this dog thing, but I don't like it. I have enough people and problems to contend with at Homicide without coming home to them at night."

"I know," Matt said instantly. "I'm really sorry. It was a stupid thing to do—telling them where I lived. I won't do it again." From now on, as long as I'm living with you, he promised the lieutenant silently, I'll either keep out of trouble or handle it on my own.

Ryder was looking around for something to flick his cigarette ash into. Finding nothing suitable, he went down to his own bedroom for an ashtray, giving Matt time to think ahead. If Ryder asked him not to cause any more trouble about the dog, what was he going to do?

He knew what he would have done in the old days— plowed straight ahead and worried about the consequences afterwards—but old Damn-the-Torpedoes McKendrick had been blasted out of the water for good. He had a choice, but it was as lousy a choice as you could get.

If Ryder told him to drop this, and he did, the dog would go on menacing people. One day, if it didn't go after him, it might attack Will or his little brother. And if he didn't drop it, if he got himself into more trouble over Boo, Ryder could say to hell with it and change his mind about wanting him to live with them.

"Matt?" Ryder was back and apparently waiting for an answer.

"Sorry, sir, I didn't hear you."

"I said, what are you planning to do now?"

Matt swallowed nervously. He wished he could read the lieutenant's mind or even his face at this moment, but Ryder's thoughts, as always, were too well hidden. "Sir, I wish I could promise you there won't be any more trouble with the dog. If it was just me who was having a problem, I could, but the dog's a danger to ev—"

Ryder swore. "Matt, I've heard all I want to about that damned dog for one night. I believe you when you tell me he's a nuisance, but his owners claim he's not bothering anyone else." He stopped, eyeing Matt thoughtfully. The silence lengthened.

What are you thinking? Matt asked him silently. Are you wishing you could handcuff me to the bed or lock me in a cage in the attic? Wishing you'd never set eyes on me; never brought me home with you; never asked me to stay? Or are you looking ahead and wondering if it's going to be one damn thing after another? Thinking you'd be better off turning me loose and letting me fend for myself now that the cast is gone and I'm well enough to be out looking for trouble again?

Ryder made a sudden sound—part laugh, part groan.

"Sir?" Matt said tensely.

The lieutenant laughed. "Remind me to tell you sometime. Look, Matt, this is your problem, and I expect you to handle it any way you think best. Is that all right with you?"

Is that all ri—? No "Do what I tell you, or else"? No having to choose between saving his own skin and saving someone else's? Matt's taut muscles relaxed with such swiftness, he was glad he was sitting down. "Yes . . . okay," he mumbled. "I guess so."

"Right. If you find you do need me, though, I'm available." Ryder stood, stretching. "Oh, before I forget—Tony said to tell you he'll pick you up tomorrow about seven. Good night, Matt," he added, smiling himself in response to Matt's sudden all-out grin. "Enjoy your sail."

"I will, sir. Thanks. Thanks a lot!" If there was any way to solve the problem of Boo without bringing Ryder into it again, he would find it. That was a promise too.

8

Monday morning Matt turned up Las Lomas at a quarter
to seven. Armed with a plastic water pistol of Michael's
that he had filled with a mild solution of ammonia and
water, he was hoping that the dog would be chained in its
backyard or have undergone a drastic change in its person-
ality. Boo was waiting for him in the bushes.

Matt held off until the snarling animal was three feet
away, then squirted him repeatedly in the face. Not even
Boo was crazy enough to ignore the effects of the stinging
solution. Snapping at the air, he turned tail and fled to the
safety of his front lawn, where he thrust his nose into the
damp grass and rolled frantically to rid himself of the terrible smell.

Once safely past the dog's territory, Matt could let himself feel sorry for Boo. The solution was weak, but getting
it in the face ranked right up there with being scored on
by an angry skunk. When he told Will about his new tac-
tic, Will congratulated him on his sheer genius.

"Rocks are only going to make him worse," he pointed

out, "but this way you might be able to teach him the street doesn't belong to him after all."

They decided to try the entire figure eight that morning, pedaling steadily without conversation until they came back out on Las Lomas above the Schuylers' house. Racing each other the last hundred yards, they collapsed in the family room a few minutes later, and some time passed before Will was able to heave himself off the floor and stagger into the kitchen.

"I'm starving," he said. "You had any breakfast yet?"

"No, but that's okay. I'll have to eat no matter what time I get back. Mrs. B will see to that."

"Mrs. B?"

"Housekeeper, I guess you'd call her. But she's more like a resident grandmother."

"Oh. Sounds good." Will suddenly seemed very busy banging around in cupboards. "Wish we had one. How about some orange juice? Or Energade?"

Matt had heard of the athletes' drink but never tasted it. "I'll try the Energade, I guess. Thanks."

Lew Schuyler burst into the room, threw Matt a casual "Hi!" as if he had known him all his life, and slid onto the piano bench, tentatively touching the keys. Will set two frosty glasses in front of Matt and emptied the contents of a large white envelope on the table.

"Seems too bad to spoil a perfectly nice day," he said cheerfully, "but I figured you'd want to know the worst about the high school. This is the stuff they sent the sophomores a while back. Meg's course catalogue is here somewhere, too."

While they rummaged through the leaflets and letters, and Matt tried to get a feeling for the school, Lew kept interrupting them to ask questions about the piano notes and how to read the music. Yielding finally to Lew's pleas, Will joined him on the bench and began to pick out a very basic tune from the beginner's book in front of them. He did not sound any better than his little brother.

"Sing it," Lew suggested, reading the chatty instructions at the top of the page. It was immediately obvious that the instructions had not been written with a fifteen-year-old's froggy bass voice in mind.

Staring open-mouthed as Will rumbled his way through "Fun-ny mon-key at-the-zoo. How-de do . . . how-de-do," Lew let out a shriek of laughter and fell backwards off the piano bench with a thud that made Matt wince. Clutching his stomach, he rolled across the floor laughing wildly and crowing, "How-de-do!" whenever he had breath to spare. Gulping down a few snorts of his own, Matt tried to concentrate on the course catalogue.

Ignoring them, Will turned the page. "Hush, my sweety," he crooned, plinking away. "Ba-by's slee-ping."

"I'm trying, I'm trying," Lew howled from under the table. Abandoning the catalogue, Matt buried his face in a pillow. A moment later he was on the floor himself, brought down by Will's solemn, one-note rendition of Red Fox, the Indian boy "—who would play . . . on his tom-tom, night and day."

"Tom-tom-tom!" wailed Lew, his face a violent shade of purple. "He must have driven everybody mad!"

Will rose from the piano bench and acknowledged his

prostrate audience with a sweeping bow. "Zank you, zank you," he intoned in a thick professorial accent. "And vor ze next numbair, ve vill prezent—" He paused dramatically. "Zee Beeg Bull Frog!"

Stunned silence greeted this announcement, followed by thuds, crashes, and bellows for help as Matt and Lew threw themselves on Will and wrestled him to the floor. A moment later everything screeched to a halt as an irritated female voice demanded to know what they were doing.

Matt sat up in sudden panic, expecting to see Mrs. Schuyler. Instead, a girl was standing in the doorway. Small and slightly built, her blonde hair and green eyes reminded him strongly of Lew, but the exasperated expression on her face made her look nineteen or twenty at least.

"What does it look like we're doing?" Will said calmly, sitting up himself. "We're playing the piano obviously."

"Oh, is that all it is?" she said with exaggerated relief. "Well, I'm glad you weren't wrestling or something. The whole house would have probably collapsed!"

Will grinned at Matt. "My sister, the dragon lady," he said in an audible aside that made her blush. "This is Meg," he added quickly. "The horse freak."

"Oh . . . hi." Matt propelled himself rapidly to his feet. "I'm Matt." No *McKendrick* in case they'd heard the name before. Just Matt. *McKendrick, you are such a—!*

"Hi," she said. The hair curling gypsylike around her face and the sudden smile reflected in her eyes made her look much younger, and as impish as her little brother.

He grinned back involuntarily. Five down, he was thinking, and only four to go. Every time he met another one

66

of the nine-out-of-ten who didn't remember him, he dreaded the inevitable meeting with number ten even more. After that it would be all over.

"Meg, this is the guy I was telling you about," Will was explaining. "He wanted to know about renting horses at the stable."

Meg gave Matt an appraising glance that seemed in some mysterious way to find him lacking. "Do you ride?"

"Western," he said shortly, annoyed by her patronizing attitude, and added as an idea started to bloom, "a little."

"They don't have rentals, but a lot of the horses need exercising. People are on vacation right now. Can you handle a horse in a ring?"

"I guess so." The idea blossomed into a plan. He would show Will's bossy sister that it wasn't safe to make assumptions about people you didn't know. "Even if I did fall off —in a ring the horse couldn't go anywhere, could it?"

"No-o-o." She drew the sound out doubtfully as if she were sorry she had mentioned the idea in the first place.

"When can I come?" he said quickly, afraid she was about to change her mind.

"I'm going up there now. If you want to come, I guess it's all right."

Matt considered his cutoffs, his running shoes, and the cavernous hollow normally inhabited by his stomach. Not the right conditions either inside or out to be starting on a morning ride. Then he thought about the prospect of showing Miss Know-It-All a thing or two and finally about the feel of a horse under him again. "I'll come," he said firmly.

That settled, she turned to Will and Lew. "Will you two

please get busy on that side yard before Dad comes home tonight?"

"It's too hot," Lew complained. He was lying on his back on the floor, shooting rubber bands at the light fixture.

"You've been saying it's too hot ever since he asked you last week. Just do it and get it over with."

Will winked at Matt. "My sister, the slave driver. Come on, Annie Oakley," he added, nudging Lew with his foot. "Work time."

"Who's Annie Oakley?" Lew was asking as the two of them went out the sliding glass door.

Will stuck his head inside again a second later to wish Matt luck and remind him about meeting in the morning and vanished for good. Matt was left with Meg, a prospect he didn't relish. She was straightening up the mess they'd made, giving each pillow a sharp *thwack!* before putting it back on the sofa as if she resented having to do it.

"Do you mind if I call home first?" he said.

"No," she said shortly, gathering the scattered high school papers together. "The phone's on the wall by the sink. I'm not coming home until two," she added, but not until after he had left the message with Michael and hung up.

"That's okay." If she was trying to get rid of him, she'd have to do better than that. "I know the way back. I can walk."

"Okay, then." She scooped her wallet and a set of car keys off the countertop. "Let's go."

9

For most of the ride out to the stable they preserved a prickly silence. Meg drove so cautiously that Matt, who had been driving on the ranch since he was ten, was tempted several times to comment. When she came to a complete stop while a squirrel made up its mind whether to cross the road, he could not keep silent any longer.

"How long have you had your license?" he said with barely concealed sarcasm.

"Three weeks."

Three weeks? That silenced him. She was only a month older than he was. Her "I'm in charge here" attitude made her seem a lot older. Well, as long as she could get him into the stable, he decided, she could be anything she liked.

After twenty minutes with the horses he had to admit that, whatever else she might be, she was a good teacher. All the time she was grooming, saddling, and bridling an elderly chestnut for him, she was giving him the hows and whys of everything she did in words of one syllable. If he had been the six-year-old beginner she seemed to think he was, he would have learned a lot.

Although impatient to get on with the ride, he was more determined now than ever to wait for the right dramatic moment to reveal the joke and submitted meekly while she led his horse to the arena, helped him mount, and tried unsuccessfully to lengthen the stirrups for him. Leaving him with instructions to walk the chestnut four times around the ring in both directions, she went to get Cricket, her half-Arab gelding.

While she was gone, Matt let himself relax, riding with his feet out of the stirrups, which were too short to be of any use. Enjoying the homely smells of leather and horseflesh, the sun's warmth on his head, and the rhythmic swaying of his body in response to the horse's plodding steps— he did not notice the man leaning on the rail watching him until he had completed his sixth circuit.

Not a man, he realized as he rode past, but a guy older than he was, and bigger, with a steady gaze and a grin on his wide mouth that made Matt nervous. He doesn't know who I am, he reassured himself, or he wouldn't be grinning. Maybe he's guessed I'm playing games with Meg.

When she rode into the arena a few minutes later, Matt watched the two of them closely. The guy nodded at her, and she nodded back, but neither one said anything. Matt slumped in the saddle and tried to look more like a novice horseman.

Meg took Cricket around the arena a few times at a brisk walk before catching up with Matt to explain how to handle the jog. "I'm going to be going faster than you because I'm riding English style, and the trot is easier to post to if you speed it up. Don't try to keep up with us, okay?"

"Okay," he said, noticing that her face had completely lost the peevish expression that had rubbed him the wrong way at first. She was obviously a lot happier at the stables than she was at home.

Clutching the saddle horn for appearance's sake, he started off, finding that looking awkward and uncomfortable was easier than he'd anticipated. The horse had such uneven gaits, it was like riding a jackhammer. Tired of the charade he was playing, he wished he could think of a way to end it gracefully. By the time he had done a few circuits at the jog and then at the lope, he decided there was no way out of this predicament except a humble confession, and he wasn't desperate enough for that yet.

Meg's friend had disappeared at some point. Matt and Meg were walking their horses when the guy came back leading a palomino with a wall-eye. At the gate it threw its head back against the bit, its rump skittering nervously from side to side. Matt instantly sized this one up as a much bigger handful than the chestnut.

"This baby hasn't been exercised in a long time," Meg said dubiously. "I'm not sure I should let you try him."

The doubting note in her voice was all he needed. "I think I've got the hang of it now," he assured her. "I'll give that one a good workout." He slid off his placid mount and handed her the reins.

"This one is called Buster," Meg's friend said. His words were slow and precise, reminding Matt of someone else. Someone he used to know? The guy's big hands were firm and gentle at Buster's head as he led the palomino into the arena and held him while Matt mounted. The stirrups were long enough this time, and it was lucky they were.

If Buster had been exercised by anyone in the last year, it hadn't made much impression. He took off at a dead run for the far fence. Holding him straight at it, Matt pulled him up so suddenly that Buster was almost sitting down. Gathering himself together, the palomino lunged forward, hopping and bucking his way down the center of the ring. When Matt refused to let him drop his head any-more, Buster reared and threw his head back, but Matt was ready for this maneuver and slapped him sharply between the ears.

Several more minutes were wasted on this nonsense be-fore Buster calmed down to the point where Matt could do something with him. Moving the palomino out at a walk, he circled the arena a couple of times while he got himself under control. This crazy horse wasn't fit for a beginner to ride—maybe not fit for anyone to ride. What the Sam Hill did Meg and her funny friend think they were trying to pull?

He rode up to the other two and stopped, scowling furi-ously, while the trembling Buster pawed restlessly at the shavings underfoot. Before he could say anything, Meg ex-changed a look with her buddy and began to laugh. The guy did not share her amusement. Big as he was, he was watching Matt nervously.

"What kind of a crazy stunt was that to pull?" Matt yelled over Meg's laughter. "This is no horse for a begin-ner."

Looking more like her mischievous little brother every second, Meg caught her breath. "No, he's not," she agreed, "but you're no beginner, either."

She had him cold. Matt felt his righteous anger fizzle away. "How did you know?" he said sheepishly.

"Well, for one thing, your hands give you away. Don saw that right from the start." Don nodded. He was smiling again. "No beginner has that constant light contact with the horse's mouth that you do. And the other thing—" Meg giggled. "You rode the chestnut without stirrups through the whole workout. Lope and all!"

"Oh lord, I forgot all about them!" Matt began laughing himself. "You're right. I lived on a ranch most of my life. I guess it's not that easy to pretend you don't know how to do something when you've been doing it since you were three."

Matt's usefulness established, the three of them groomed and exercised nine other horses before Matt caught sight of the time on the cobwebby clock in the tackroom and told the other two he had to go. "Mrs. B will think I died of starvation if I don't turn up soon. And she could be right," he added as his long-neglected stomach said a very rude word.

"You can call from here," Don said. "There's a pay phone. I can lend you a dime."

"Maybe I'd better." What he really wanted was to call out somewhere for a pizza. Home delivery guaranteed in twenty minutes. Help! his stomach bellowed. Emergency! Emergency!

"Don't bother to call," Meg said, laughing at his anguished expression. "I'll take you home. I'm ready to leave, too."

"Are you coming tomorrow?" Don asked in his deliberate way.

Matt looked at Meg. "Will the owners mind?"

"Not you, they won't. Mr. Santini told Don you were welcome to come whenever you wanted."

"Is he still around? Maybe I should say hello or something." And then good-bye? Sometimes he wished he would meet up with number ten and get it over with so he could stop worrying about it.

"Do it tomorrow," Meg said, to his immense relief. He didn't really want everything to end. Not yet. "Once you get him talking," she explained, "he won't quit until he's shown you the whole stable and told you the history and bad habits of every horse in it."

"If I'm going to be riding with you two," Matt said, needling them a little, "I could use a rundown on the horses' bad habits."

"You aren't still mad, are you?" Don said anxiously. A funny question for someone his age to be asking.

Matt looked at the strong face under its shock of brown hair. Don's worried eyes met his with the directness of someone nearer Lew Schuyler's age.

"No," Matt said slowly. Who was it the guy reminded him of? He and Meg were halfway home before it occurred to him to ask her about Don.

"There's nothing wrong with him, if that's what you're thinking," Meg said, instantly on the defensive.

Her words jogged his memory. He had said exactly the

74

same thing himself about Rainey Clay. They had kept Rainey back so much in Craigie that by high school he was two years older than everybody else and still about three years behind.

"I knew a guy like Don once," he said slowly, thinking about the fight he had gotten into defending Rainey. The way his temper had blazed out of control then had come back to haunt him when Ryder and Sheriff Hensley were trying to decide whether he could have accidentally killed his own sister.

"He's slow, that's all," Meg said. "Once he learns something, he doesn't forget it. It just takes him longer. He's turning eighteen in December, and they're graduating him in January, even though he's still somewhere around fifth-grade level when it comes to math or reading.

"But give him an animal—any animal, not just horses—and he's got something they can't teach you in school." She hit the wheel with her first, and the car swerved. "Sorry," she said. "It's just that it's such a stupid waste! There's nothing he can't do with animals. Sometimes I think he can almost talk to them. But he lives with a foster mother who thinks he's dumb. She thinks he can't ever get a job—that's why she's made him stay in school so long—and she won't help him try."

Meg had stopped the car in her driveway by this time, but neither of them moved. Why do people do such lousy things to each other? Matt was thinking. He opened his door. "At least the guy I knew had a family," he said heavily. "They liked him the way he was. Well, thanks. Thanks a lot."

Meg shook herself. "Anytime," she said. "Oh wait! I forgot to take you home."

"That's okay. I can get there fast enough on my own." Did she mean that *anytime*? He was afraid to ask, afraid she was just being polite, but she gave him the answer herself.

"When do you and Will usually get through bicycling?"

"Around eight, eight-thirty."

"I don't usually leave for the stables before nine-thirty anyway because of—well, things I have to do first."

"Great!" Matt said. "Then I can have breakfast."

So it was all arranged. Astonished by his incredible luck, Matt did not realize until after he got home that Boo had not challenged him on his way past. Talking nonstop through lunch, he described the Schuylers and his day at the stable to Michael, Jenny, and Mrs. B, and at dinner went through his day all over again for Sally and Ryder. Eagerly accepting their suggestion that he ask the Schuylers for a swim some afternoon, he went to bed so high on the day's happenings and the prospect of more to come, that not even the specter of Boo was enough to bring him down before he fell asleep.

10

The days that followed rapidly shook themselves down into a routine. Armed with his ammonia-water mixture, Matt passed Boo's house every morning about seven. Each morning Boo was waiting in the bushes, but by Thursday he was definitely less enthusiastic about attacking. Matt decided Will's theory about teaching him to stay off the street might be working out.

After bicycling strenuously for an hour or so, he went home to change and have breakfast and was back at the Schuylers' a little after nine. He spent the rest of the morning at the stables with Don and Meg, the stable's owner having proved to be number seven on his mental countdown of nine and one, and the hot afternoons in the pool with Michael and Jenny—and Sally when she wasn't out on a photography or writing assignment.

The only part of the day he did not enjoy was being in the Schuyler house when Meg was there. At the stable she was full of mischief, did her share of the heavy, dirty chores uncomplainingly, and worked with the horses in a thoroughly professional way that Matt admired. At home she was tense, irritable, and bossy, as if the entire responsibility for keeping the house going rested on her. Although Will had an apparently inexhaustible supply of teasing nicknames for her, Matt noticed he did whatever she asked him without protest and usually managed to con Lew into doing his share as well. Not having met either of their parents yet, Matt wondered what was wrong with Mrs. Schuyler for Meg to be acting as chief housekeeper. On Friday he found out.

He was in the family room playing Blackjack with Lew while waiting for Meg. The front door slammed, something heavy was dropped on the tile floor, and a voice screamed, "That stupid Pam—I hate her! I'm never going to speak to her again!"

"Oh boy," Lew said softly. "Here we go again."

Matt had not met the fourth member of the Schuyler family, eleven-year-old Carey, because she was always at swimming practice when he came in the morning. Having seen her arm once hurling a tennis ball and heard her screeching at Lew, he did not feel he was missing much.

Shouting "Where's Will?" she came storming down the hall toward the family room and stopped in the doorway, blushing furiously when she saw Matt. In the Schuyler family, Lew and Meg were look-alikes, and Carey, with her dark blonde hair and deep brown eyes, was a miniature double for Will.

"Having his tennis lesson," Lew reminded her. "You want another card?" he said to Matt.

"Uh . . . no." When Matt glanced up again, Carey

had vanished. Moments later sounds of a violent argument carried up the hall.

"Girls. . . ." Lew sighed heavily. "Sisters!" he added, as if the burden were too much to bear. "I win again," he said, perking up momentarily. As the sounds of battle continued, he began shuffling the cards with great precision, avoiding Matt's eye. "I wish they wouldn't fight," he muttered.

They really were fighting. It erupted into the hall, and they heard Carey's wail, "I wish Mom were here instead of you," and Meg's fierce, "Well so do I, you little brat, but she's not!"

Meg appeared a moment later, breathing hard. Two angry red spots burned in her cheeks, and the rest of her face was pale. "Let's get out of here," she said. Hastily challenging Lew to a rematch on Monday, Matt went.

Meg did not calm down until she had a brush in her hand and was giving Cricket the grooming of his life. "I'm sorry," she said suddenly.

Matt peered over Buster's dusty withers. Her back was to him; all he could see was her wildly curling hair and the twin ridges of her shoulder blades standing out sharply under her T-shirt. "What?"

"About this morning. I try not to come apart like that very often. It's just that sometimes—" She broke off.

Matt didn't see anything so unusual about sisters fighting and said so.

"That's okay if you're just sisters." Meg found a spot on Cricket's far side that needed special attention. "Only I'm not just her sister." Silence. "I'm the closest thing she's got to a mother now, too."

There were several possible reasons why there was no Mrs. Schuyler. Matt had no way of guessing which was the right one, and he was not about to ask.

"She died." Meg's voice was muffled in Cricket's flanks. "Last spring. Drowned. Trying to save a kid she never saw before in her life from a wild river."

Oh lord, Meg . . . you loved her, too, didn't you? How can people die when they're loved so much? And needed, damn it! Wanting her to know he understood, he spoke without thinking. "My mom died last March in a car crash. My dad, too."

Their eyes met briefly, sharing each other's pain. An instant later Don exploded. "That's the lousiest deal I ev—!"

He stopped abruptly, the uncharacteristic anger in his voice surprising all of them. Suddenly everyone was very busy saddling and bridling and getting on with the exercising. Nobody mentioned the subject again. Nobody had much to say all morning, in fact.

They were on their way home when Meg let out a long sigh. "That's Don for you," she said. She did not have to elaborate.

"Thinking we were the ones who had the lousy deal?"

"Yes. When he never had anyone, not even for a while. Just some county home, and then his awful foster mother."

Not to have had all those years with his mom and dad and Katie? No way. Even if it meant he would not have had to live through the last six months—or the next six— he would not have traded places with Don.

They were pulling into the driveway when Meg asked if he was busy that evening.

"No. Why?"

"We're all going to the movies. Want to come?"

He should have seen it coming and ducked, said he was babysitting or something. Now there was no way out. Either he stuck his neck out a whole lot farther than he'd done up to now and prayed his luck would hold, or he told Meg here and now who he was. The one way there was a chance nothing would happen, and his friendship with the Schuylers could keep going for a while. The other way he would bring the friendship and everything else to a screaming halt. "I'll take the chance," he said.

"What?"

"I'll come," he said hastily. "What time?"

"We'll pick you up at six."

"Great!" Matt said enthusiastically to cover his earlier slip of the tongue. Promptly at six he found himself in the Schuyler station wagon again, heading down Verde Canyon with his fingers crossed and wishing for the first time in his life that he were eight inches shorter and not so visible in a crowd.

Because Will was in top form, the evening got off to a flying start. Everyone, including Matt, felt sick from laughing long before they reached the theater complex. The ticket lines for the five theaters were all long ones, and as they found the end of the line they wanted, Will began outlining a cartoon idea for Lew, who drew comic books in his spare time. Matt thrust his fists into the pockets of his jeans so no one could see his white knuckles and sent a swift glance around the theater lobby. One look was all he needed to tell him his luck had run out.

Two lines over was number ten, the guy who remembered him from the papers last spring. He was shorter than Matt, but heftier, and Matt had seen the girl's horrified expression as his glance flicked over them. The guy was telling her who he was.

Matt broke into a cold sweat. Now what? What if they marched over and said, "Hey, aren't you the one who killed a little girl last spring and got away with it?" What could he say? Not yes. That was the one thing no one had ever been able to make him say, and no one ever would. If he refused to answer them at all, tried to ignore them, they'd think he was admitting his guilt like someone taking the Fifth Amendment. The only answer he could give was *no*.

What if they wouldn't accept it? What if they insisted they were right and argued with him, and other people crowded around to see what was happening? What if someone else in the crowd remembered him and shouted out, "Hey, yeah, I remember that story. That's the guy all right."

Then what? The scene of his nightmares? Shouts, insults, threats? But this time he wasn't alone. The Schuylers would be trapped in it with him.

Jesus—! How could he have been so stupid? Hiding behind Ryder and Tony was one thing—they were cops and used to handling crowds. But the Schuylers were just friends. He never should have gotten them mixed up in this. He could see it now—Carey terrified, Lew lost in the jostling mob, Will and Meg trying to protect them and yelling that they didn't know anything about it because he hadn't told them who he was. And nobody listening to them either. *Do something, McKendrick! Get yourself out out of here before it's too—*

"Hey, Matt, where are you going? It's this way. Number two."

"I—uh . . . oh, yeah." Matt gave Lew a half-hearted grin and glanced back over his shoulder. The guy and his girl had already bought their tickets and disappeared.

"Matt, are you okay?" Meg said. "You look kind of white."

"White . . . ? Uh, no . . . no, I'm okay." As the realization that he was safe—that the nightmare wasn't going to happen—swept through him, his mood swung wildly to elation. He was safe! They were all safe! Nothing was changed!

Like someone recovering from a close brush with death, he began taking an enormous delight in being alive, fully prepared to enjoy every minute that was left of this night out. It wasn't hard to do. From the moment they settled into their seats, the night became as hilariously unpredictable as anything he had ever experienced in Sally's company.

Five minutes before the film started, they were surrounded suddenly by the sounds of coins—lots of coins—dropping and rolling across the floor beneath their feet.

"Lew . . ." Meg said ominously. "Don't tell me you brought all your change with you again."

"Hey, Lew," Will added. "If you're throwing it around, how about tossing some my way?"

But Lew was already on the floor, scrabbling desperately under the seats for his life's savings with a sympathetic Carey on her knees beside him. The three bigger ones picked up all the coins they could reach from their seats, and Lew and Carey were retrieving the last few stragglers from under the row in front of them when an enormous woman sitting in front of Will suddenly jerked and let out a scream that silenced the whole theater.

"Rats!" she yelled. "There are rats in this theater! I just felt one run past my leg!"

Grabbing for shirts, Will and Meg had Lew and Carey back in their seats an instant before the usher came rushing to her rescue. Getting down on hands and knees himself, he examined the entire theater from floor level before she would accept his assurance that there were no rats and never had been. It was not until his perspiring face rose above the line of seats again that he caught sight of the five suspiciously red faces in the row behind her.

From his expression an embarrassing scene was shaping up fast, with the five of them in the starring roles. Exposure and expulsion were seconds away. But as the first helpless giggle escaped from a scarlet-faced Carey, the lights dimmed. They were saved . . . for the moment.

Unfortunately the movie they had come to see had an unusually quiet sound track. Every stir and rustle the audience made seemed to echo through the small theater, and judging by the sounds they were making, three of the patrons would have been better off if they'd stayed home in bed.

One of them had a high twittering sneeze like a cat's.

84

One blew his nose every two or three minutes—a loud honk followed by a series of little snorts and sniffles. And a man directly behind Will had coughing fits that started with a roar and ended with a whoop and a gasp as if he were strangling.

Throughout the first hour of the film, this trio played its instruments like a German band, while Matt and the four Schuylers held their noses, bit their lips, and tried frantically to keep the lid on their laughter. If they had been the only ones who were finding it funny, they might have survived; but they weren't. Somewhere at the back of the theater, someone suddenly let out a thin squeal. It was hastily cut off, but the damage was done. All over the theater tiny squeaks and chirps began escaping from behind people's hands in an infectious epidemic that for the five of them proved fatal.

Lew administered the *coup de grace*, choosing that moment to whisper something to Will, who gave it to Matt, between convulsive gasps, as "Hybid gnat lady neber gums packer uggan!" Matt managed to pass this on—one agonizing word at a time—to Meg, who delivered it, squeaking and snuffling in her ear, to Carey. When Carey leaned forward and said in a pained whisper, "What was that again?" Matt thought he was going to pass out if he couldn't stop choking back his howls and breathe.

"Oh lord!" he gasped, lurching to his feet. "I can't stand any more of this. I'll wait for you guys outside."

Without a word, the four Schuylers rose and stumbled after him. Once outside, the five of them staggered around on the sidewalk holding each other up and howling help-

lessly until their stomachs untied the knots the last tor-
tured hour had tied in them.

It wasn't until they were on their way home that someone finally asked about the unintelligible message they'd
received. Once Lew explained that the squeaky bursts of
laughter had sounded so much like mice he had said to
Will, "I bet that rat lady never comes back here again!"
everyone had to tell everyone else what they thought they'd
heard. They were still hiccuping weakly when they drew
up in the Ryders' drive.

"We should have gone to Leonard's afterwards for ice
cream," Meg said as Matt was getting out, "only with our
stomachs in such bad shape, I thought it wasn't such a
good idea."

"Maybe next time," Matt said. As the Schuyler station
wagon backed away from him down the drive, taking with
it all the warmth of the last week and their crazy night together, he added under his breath, "—if there is one."

The time had come for him to face facts. And the fact
was that the Schuylers had to know who he was. Not for
his sake. For theirs.

11

Because Mr. Schuyler's job as a lawyer kept him working late almost every night, he usually took his family somewhere on the weekends to make up for it. For two days Matt saw none of the Schuylers. It gave him plenty of time to think about the problems he had created by not telling them who he was from the beginning. As soon as he knew he might be seeing them again, he should have gotten everything out in the open and let them decide whether they wanted to go on seeing him or tell him to get lost.

He had been worrying so much about the tenth guy who would know who he was already, he hadn't realized that his real problem was going to be with the nine guys who would have to be told. And they would have to be—all of them. Starting with the Schuylers. Last night had showed him this all too clearly.

Anyone who made friends with him was taking a risk. Even if it meant losing friends as fast as he made them, he could not put people in that position without warning them first. The Schuylers had to know. He could delay the moment of truth a little by refusing any more invitations to go out in public with them, but the longer he put it off, the greater the chance grew of their hearing about him from someone else. If he wanted them to have the real story, he would have to tell them himself, and he would have to do it soon.

Knowing what had to be done, and doing it, were two entirely different things. In spite of his determination to get everything out in the open, Monday passed without giving him the chance, although it brought with it such a heat wave that he asked the Schuylers down in the afternoon for a swim. Tuesday came and went the same way. He wanted to tell all of them at one time, but it wasn't easy to find a time when they were all at home together. He began to think he never would.

His other problem, Boo, had become by then only a minor irritation; his success with the ammonia-water had convinced him he had discouraged the dog from attacking anyone on the street. On Wednesday, he discovered he was wrong.

Because he and Will were starting earlier to beat the heat, Matt turned up Las Lomas in time to see the paper boy on his bicycle hurl a rolled-up newspaper at the Kennetts' front door. Instantly Boo launched himself out of the shrubbery to defend his family from this imagined assault.

Boo's flying attack knocked boy and bike halfway across the street. Before they hit the ground, the dog was going for the boy's throat. Screaming in pain and terror, the boy tried to beat him off, but the dog was too strong. Locking its teeth in the boy's arm, it tore at him like a thing gone mad.

Racing toward them, Matt screamed too—cursing the dog and yelling for help. Grabbing the dog's collar with some idea of choking it into unconsciousness, he yanked on the chain with all his strength.

The next moments were chaos—the boy's screams mingling with Matt's desperate yells; a white-faced Will taking the Kennetts' steps four at a time, keeping one hand on the doorbell while he pounded on the door; Kennett himself struggling furiously with the crazed dog, while his wife stood by uselessly wringing her hands and wailing, "I don't believe it. Oh my God, I don't believe it!"; Will telling the boy to hang on, they had called his mother, she was coming, hang on. . . .

Finally, in desperation, Kennett forced a jack handle between the dog's teeth and jerked down on it. There was a sharp crack. Boo howled. The boy screamed too, but his arm was free, the skin bruised and torn. Blood began to ooze and then stream from a dozen punctures, while something white and shiny bulged up through a deep ragged tear.

Matt's stomach heaved as Will gagged and turned away. Kennett was wrestling the dog into the garage when a car skidded to a halt across the road and a woman ran over. She was followed by a guy in his twenties.

"Darren!" she cried, terrified. "Darren, what happened?" The older boy was helping his brother to his feet.

"I—I just tossed the paper," Darren sobbed. "Into their

89

yard, Mom. Just tossed the paper. And he came—came after me."

Darren's mother turned wildly on Mrs. Kennett. "Why didn't you get rid of that monster? I warned you he was dangerous, and you—"

"I'm sorry," Mrs. Kennett wailed. "I didn't know. I'm so sorry."

The woman and her two sons were getting in the car when Will came to life. "I'll keep Darren's bike in our garage, Mrs. Kwan," he called out. The older brother, sitting in the back with Darren, nodded at them as the car accelerated and raced off. It turned right on Verde Canyon without stopping.

Newspapers were scattered all over the road. Grateful for something to do, Matt and Will picked them up and pushed Darren's bike up the street to the Schuylers'. Behind them, Kennett was yelling at his wife to quit standing there like a dummy and call Animal Control. Boo was still howling.

They were bumping the bike down the steps when Matt roused himself. "I'm glad it wasn't Lew . . . or you," he said awkwardly. He was haunted by the memory of calves he had seen after they had been killed and savaged by dog packs. "What if we hadn't been there? What if I'd done something about Boo last week? It never would have—"

"Don't!" Will was shaking. "It doesn't do any good. Come on, let's get going before I come completely unglued."

Pedaling furiously for the next hour and a half, they came back to the Schuylers' to find Meg vacuuming in the living room and Lew in the kitchen eating a bowl of cereal. Life going on as if nothing had happened.

"Hey, Will," Lew said as soon as they walked in. "Some guy wanted you. He said it was about Boo."

Will groaned. "Now what? Haven't we heard enough about Boo to last us the rest of our— Who was he? Did he say?"

"No. He gave me his card, though." Lew extracted a business card from his hip pocket. "Brian Bellacosi," he read. "Animal Control Department. Los Angeles Coun—"

"Okay, okay," Will interrupted him, laughing. "The kid's a walking computer. Ask him a question, and you get it *all* back. Let's have the card," he added. "I guess I'll call him and get it over with. Here, Matt." Will pushed a giant glass of orange juice across the counter at him and dialed the number.

After he reached the right person, he said, "I don't know," three times in a row before motioning to Matt. "The guy who saw it all is right here, if you want to talk to him. Okay." Nodding, he held out the phone.

The man on the other end wanted details. Had Darren threatened the dog or provoked it in any way? Matt told him exactly what he had seen, and about his own experiences with Boo in the past weeks.

"It sounds like a pretty clear-cut case, then. The dog will have to be destroyed." The man thanked him for his help. "Now, I'll need your name and address for the report."

His name and—? Matt glanced around. Will and Lew were at the table. Meg was sitting at the piano, lightly fingering the keys. They were all within earshot. The moment he had been waiting for was on him. In a few minutes he'd be telling the Schuylers everything, and a few minutes later they'd be telling him good-bye. So much for all his brave resolutions in the darkness of his bedroom. What he wanted to do right now was slam the phone down and run.

"First name?" the man repeated.

"Uh, Matt—Matthew," he stammered.

"Last name?"

"McKendrick." What was happening behind him? Was Will frowning, wondering where he'd heard that name before? Was Meg staring at him, the angry color beginning to flare across her cheekbones? Oh lord—

"Can you spell that for me?"

Sure. Just in case they didn't catch it the first time. Mister, you don't know what you're doing to me. "M-little c-K-e-n-d-r-i-c-k." While he was giving the man his address, he stared at the Schuylers' phone list on the wall in front of him. His name had been added in blue felt pen, the Ryders' number beside it. As he was hanging up, he looked more closely at it, thinking he saw a line drawn through his name, but it was only one of the lines printed on the back of the paper.

Are you planning on becoming a permanent fixture? he asked himself a moment later. *A hat rack or something? Quit standing here with your face to the wall, McKendrick, and get this thing over with.*

He swung around and straightened up. "I guess you heard me give the man my name."

Meg was still at the piano, humming softly to herself.

Will was checking out the baseball standings in the morning paper. Only Lew seemed interested.

"I thought it was Ryder," he said as he carried his bowl and glass to the sink.

"No."

"Are you adopted?" Lew barely had the question asked before Will and Meg jumped on him and told him rudely to mind his own business.

"Wait a second, you guys," Matt said after a moment. "That's just the point. It is your business. You don't— I have to— Oh lord." He made a helpless gesture with one clenched fist. "Look, I have to tell you something I should have told you a long time ago. Do you have the time?"

"All the time in the world," Meg assured him, joining Will at the table.

Matt waited for Lew to finish putting his dishes in the dishwasher and flop expectantly into another chair before he began. He felt numb and cold, as if it were already over. Everything. The riding, the kidding around, the good times, the casual way they included him in everything they did as if he were part of the family and not just a friend from down the street. But he had survived Gary's unexpected betrayal. He should be able to cope with this. At least this time he knew what was coming.

"I'm Matt McKendrick," he said again, watching for the first telltale change in their expressions. "I'm the guy they arrested last spring for killing the little girl in the Palace Theater."

93

12

Silence.

"You're what?" Meg said blankly.

"But you didn't do it?" Lew sounded as if he wanted reassurance fast.

Will said nothing. He was avoiding Matt's eye.

It didn't look good, but he hadn't expected anything else, had he? Expected . . . no. Hoped, maybe. "No, I didn't do it. She was my sister. The trouble is, a lot of people think I did, and I'll never be able to prove I didn't. There's not enough evidence one way or the other." *Come on, you guys, ask me something. Help me out. Or is that all you need to know?* "I'm sorry I didn't tell you before. At first I didn't think it mattered, and then I was—I wanted things to stay the way they were. But you have to know so you can, you know—call it quits if you want."

"Call what quits?" Meg said sharply. She was shredding a napkin to bits with swift, angry jerks.

"With me."

"With you? What do you mean?"

Matt glanced instinctively at Will for support, but Will

had deserted him. He was turning the salt shaker slowly around and around, watching the bright pattern it made on the walls as it caught the sunlight. It reminded Matt of a prism he had once given Katie for her birthday—

To hell with it! He had known this was going to happen —why prolong the agony? "Forget it," he said bitterly. "The rest of it doesn't matter. I'm Matt McKendrick, and I guess that's all you or anybody needs to know." He took a couple of steps toward the door, but all three Schuylers instantly blocked his way.

"Wait just one minute, Matt," Meg said in her toughest I'm-in-Charge-Here voice. "It does matter."

"I don't want to call it quits," Lew was saying shrilly. "You said if we want to, and I don't want to!"

"Matt," said Will, quietly dropping his six megaton bomb. "Would it make any difference if I told you I knew who you were the first day we met?"

Voices, words, spun crazily through his head. *It does matter . . . I don't want to call it quits . . . I knew who you were the first day we met . . . Would it make any difference?*

Would it make any difference? Oh man, would it! Out of breath and shaky for the second time that day, Matt lowered himself into a chair at the table with the others. He looked at Will. Had he heard him right? "You knew who I was the first day? How come you didn't say anything?"

"What was I supposed to say?" Will was grinning a little, but Meg was still grim and pale. She looked as if she'd been given a bad scare.

You and me both, Matt told her silently. "I—well, ask

95

if I did it or something. I don't know." He was floundering. In all the confrontations he had imagined with strangers, this was the one possibility that had never crossed his mind—that someone might have read the papers and decided he was innocent!

"What good would that have done?" Will was asking. "I'd already decided you hadn't; but if I thought you had, could you have changed my mind?"

No. Will was right. Wasn't that why he was sitting here now, trying to tell them who he was? Even if they were ready to give him the benefit of the doubt, he had to warn them about all the other people who weren't. Make them understand what it was going to be like whenever he went out in public, and when he went to school.

It was crazy. The only four people he could call friends besides the Ryders and Tony and Don, and somehow he had to convince them they should tell him to get lost. "Listen, you guys," he said slowly. "I want you to know what happened—what really happened—because I don't want you to get the wrong story from someone else. And so you'll understand why most people won't feel the way you do. Afterwards, if you want to call it quits, it's okay. I'll underst—"

"I don't want to, I already said," Lew protested.

"Are you starting that again?" Meg said coldly. She was furious—no doubt about it. "Well, you listen, Matt McKendrick. I choose my own friends. Nobody, including you, tells me who I should and shouldn't like."

"Or me," Will said lightly, making an obvious effort to keep things from getting too serious. "Or should it be me

96

too? Not me? Me neither? Help!" he finished wildly. "Does anyone know *what* I mean?"

"If we're choosing," said the literal-minded Lew, refusing to be side-tracked, "I choose Matt."

"Me too," Will said at once, adding to himself, "How about that? Got it right the first time."

Meg swept the remains of the shredded napkin into a neat pile. "What are the other choices?" she said coolly.

He knew her well enough to know she was teasing. Suddenly he wanted to whoop and yell and run all the way down Verde Canyon to the bottom for the sheer unbelievable joy of being alive. *Man, am I a lucky guy!* "Clark Gable, of course," he said, equally cool. He knew whose picture was plastered all over her closet door.

"Oh . . . well, in that case," she began. "Hey, Lew, wait a minute. Matt knows I'm only jok— Help!"

Lew had heard as much of this terrible conversation as he could stand. Scrambling across the table top, he hurled himself at Meg with such force and fury that her chair went over backwards and spilled them onto the floor. Matt's and Will's efforts to rescue her turned somehow into an exuberant free-for-all tickling match, which Carey arrived home in the middle of and flung herself into with great delight. It ended finally with all of them sprawled limply on the floor of the family room like the survivors of a shipwreck, and several minutes passed before Meg was able to ask a question that got them back on the track.

"What really did happen, Matt?"

Matt heaved himself into a sitting position and propped

97

his back against the sofa. "It's going to take a while to tell you," he said apologetically.

"Don't worry," Will croaked from the corner. "You've got a captive audience. If somebody yelled 'Fire!' right now, I couldn't drag myself out of here."

It was the first time he had told this story to anyone except the police. He wasn't looking forward to it. Fixing his eyes on the opposite wall, he began with the bleak, rain-swept night when the sheriff had knocked on their door and told him about the car going off the road. He told them about the arguments, the decision to run, and the night he and Katie had arrived in Los Angeles, exhausted and hungry and broke after a week of hitching rides.

He told them about the endless day he had spent tramping the streets in a futile search for a job; about the jolting discovery that Katie wasn't in the condemned old theater building where he had left her; and about the nightmare that had begun when he was dragged into the morgue at police headquarters, forced to look at her small battered body, and then, incredibly, accused of her murder. Before he was through, Carey had burst into tears and fled.

"But, Matt," Meg protested angrily. "How could anyone believe for one second that you could have killed anybody, let alone your own sister?"

"They didn't know me or Katie. Nobody knew me. I was a stranger in L.A.—the only one around with the opportunity and no alibi, and no way to prove I hadn't done it. All I could do was keep saying it wasn't me and hope someone believed me."

"And Lieutenant Ryder did?"

98

"Not at first. Another detective, Tony Prado, was the only one who believed me from the beginning. He took me home to live with him, even though everyone was telling him he was crazy to take the risk. I couldn't stay there, though. His wife was scared of me."

"Scared? Of you?"

"She couldn't trust me. That's what I'm trying to tell you guys. Nobody in Los Angeles, once they find out who I am, is going to be able to trust me."

Will spoke for the first time. "Tell them you didn't do it, Matt. Tell them to go take a flying jump. Whatever happened to the old idea that you're innocent until you're proved guilty?"

"I don't know, but like you said before, saying I didn't do it isn't going to make anyone believe me. As long as Tony and Lieutenant Ryder can't find the guy who did kill her and prove it wasn't me, people are going to think it was. Even if they aren't sure, they're going to wonder. And as long as they aren't sure, they aren't going to be exactly overjoyed about having me around."

"Forget them, Matt! It's none of their damned business."

He had never seen Will so angry. "I can't forget them. Every time I go out of the house, I'm going to run into people. And it is their business. They think so, anyway. What if I did kill her? If I'm allowed to wander around loose, what's going to stop me from doing it again?"

"Oh come on, Matt!" Will and Meg exploded at the same time.

"I'm just telling you how it looks to them. The thing

99

is, some of them might decide to make me pay for it themselves, and if you were with me—" Meg started to interrupt, but he kept on going. "Look, you guys, it happened once before. I don't know how, or who it was anymore—by the time Lieutenant Ryder got to me, I was too far gone to tell him—but they beat me up and dumped me out in Manzanita Canyon. And the nice ordinary folks who found me the next day weren't exactly sympathetic either."

He had silenced Meg and Will, but Lew could not keep quiet any longer. "Those stupid jerks!" he yelled, grabbing a book and hurling it at the opposite wall. "If I'd been there, they would have been sorry!"

Matt grinned suddenly. He couldn't believe his luck. Pretty sure how they were going to react, he wrapped up what he had to say with a description of the couple on the ticket line the other night, and his reasons for thinking they should call it quits before school started. "I could still see you guys around here, if you want, and up at the stables."

Meg flicked her hair out of her eyes with an impatient gesture. "Are you through?" she said ominously.

"Yeah."

"Okay. Are you listening?"

"Yeah." He was puzzled by her tone.

"Lew, we're voting. Do you want to call it quits?"

"No! I keep saying it and saying it, and nobody listens to me."

"He's listening now. Will?"

"Nope."

"Me? No. Shall I get Carey back up here, or will you take my word for it that she's a no, too?"

"No—I mean, yes. Okay."

"Then," she said, symbolically dusting off her hands, "the subject is closed. Permanently," she added with a fierce scowl.

It crossed Matt's mind that she would make a great schoolteacher. He smiled at her and was rewarded with the devilish grin that made her look so young and irresponsible.

"Speaking of school—" Will said. He tossed the thought out and left Matt the option of picking up on it or letting the subject drop. Will had a knack for knowing when something might fall into the *No Trespassing* category.

Ordinarily this subject would have qualified. School was Matt's biggest problem, but he hadn't gotten very far with it on his own. "I don't know what I'm going to do about school," he said slowly. "I've thought of everything from wearing a sandwich board to making an announcement over the P.A. on the first day. Seriously, though—after you guys, I don't know what to expect anymore. Everyone will be different, but I guess I won't say anything unless they say, 'Hey, aren't you the one who—?' first. The trouble is, what do I do then? I won't say yes. I can't ignore them; and if I say no, they'll argue. I can't argue anyone into believing me."

"But you must be cleared by now, aren't you?" Meg said. "Is the case still being investigated?"

"Tony and Ryder are still working on it, but the case is officially unsolved. It's written into the record that I'm no longer a suspect, but that doesn't prove anything."

"Tell people that anyway," Will suggested. "Tell them the police record shows you're cleared. If they don't believe it, they can go downtown and look it up themselves."

Matt turned the phrase over in his mind. *The police record shows I'm cleared.* It sounded good. Flat, official, no room for debate. "It might work," he said. "Thanks. Thanks a lot you guys!" Suddenly he wanted to get moving —celebrating. "Whoo-ee!" he whooped. "Who wants to go up to the stables?"

13

In the end only Matt and Meg went; once there the heat and the flies proved a lethal combination and they were back again by noon. Before he went home, Matt asked the four Schuylers to come for a swim after lunch, and Meg had a hard time persuading Lew and Carey to give Matt a decent head start so he could get something in his stomach before they descended on the Ryders' pool like an invading army.

Meg was not as enthusiastic a swimmer as the others. No—that wasn't quite true. It was being ridden, jumped on, attacked, submerged, and half-drowned that she found less like fun and more like work than everyone else seemed to. Retreating to a lounge chair after an energetic hour or so, she combed the tangles out of her hair with her fingers and lay back, soaking up the sun and enjoying the knowledge that all those things listed on the back of the kitchen door that needed doing would just have to wait. She hadn't felt this relaxed in ages. Been digging herself deeper and deeper into a rut all summer. Housekeeping, shopping, cooking, chauffeuring—no time for anything else. Matt's coming had shaken her out of it just in time.

Shrieks and yells from the pool. She opened one eye, then the other. Lew needs a haircut, she thought, mentally adding it to the bottom of her list. Perched on Will's shoulders, he was grappling vigorously with Michael, who was riding Matt, while Carey and Jenny screamed encouragement from the sidelines. Jousting, they called it. Not one of her favorites. Against Will's 5'10" and Matt's 6'3", her 5'4" was a definite handicap. Even with Lew for a partner, she always got overpowered immediately.

Taking unfair advantage of his height, Matt was skillfully maneuvering Will toward the deep end. Suddenly Will lost his footing and sank. Shouting "Abandon ship!" Lew vanished with him in an explosion of such watery violence that it looked as if they'd been torpedoed, leaving Matt and Michael the victorious survivors of that round. Amid loud accusations of cheating and underhanded tactics, and even louder denials, new partners were chosen. The game began again.

Survivors. Will had a book called *The Survivor*, the only book he'd ever read that made him cry. That's what Matt was, a survivor. Under that reserved exterior was someone with a lot of determination and courage. She had felt that about him even before she'd found out what he had been through. It took a lot to get him down and a lot more to keep him there. Her own problems looked positively puny by comparison.

How could she have let herself get so uptight about everything this summer? For a while it had seemed as if her life was one long list of things that had to be done With things being added to the bottom faster than they were getting crossed off at the top, the list kept growing longer. She'd even had nightmares about the stupid thing coiling around and squeezing the life out of her.

Somehow having Matt around—someone who didn't need her, who gave a lot and didn't expect much back—had taken the pressure off. There wasn't one single thing she could do for him that he couldn't do as well himself. Or better. Take the horses, for example.

That first day at the stable had been so funny. He had tried so hard to look as if he didn't know what he was doing; and everything about him—the way he sat and handled the reins and moved with the horse—said he'd been doing this all his life. Maybe that was the difference. He was fun to have around. Made everybody, Carey and Lew included, feel good. Fun had kind of gotten lost in the day-to-day hassle since their mom had died.

If Dad could find somebody like Matt to distract him and make him forget himself and his problems, maybe he'd come back from that remote inner place he'd retreated to. He was so out of it, so unaware of them, that there were times since the accident when she'd felt they had lost both their parents. That's why she wanted to keep everything running smoothly, so he would always think of home as a relaxed and comfortable place to be. Someday he might be able to come back to it without its hurting so much.

This morning she'd thought they had lost Matt, too. He had scared her so badly that her first reaction had been cold rage. Like the time Lew had run into the street after one of the cats and was almost hit by a car. She could have killed him herself, once she knew he was okay.

Losing someone. You wouldn't think it would make you mad, but it does. Furious. And when you stop being angry you find out you've been bleeding to death all the time. How long does the pain last? Three months for her and still going strong. For Matt? Lord . . . forever, probably. But to look at him, you'd never guess. He was good at hiding it—that and a lot of other things he didn't want people to know. Will was, too. Better than she was. Sometimes at night when she was talking herself into hanging on for one more day, she thought she had to be the world's biggest crybaby.

A shadow fell across her face. Without opening her eyes, Meg flung out her hands to ward off the can of cold water, the wet towel, or whatever fiendish torture was about to be inflicted on her hot skin. "Don't you dare!" she said fiercely.

Someone was laughing. Not a familiar laugh. Meg opened one eye and squinted at the occupant of the chair next to hers. Oh help. . . .

"I come in peace," said the smiling, dark-haired woman. "No cold water, no slithery things down the bathing suit. You must be Meg," she added. Meg nodded, blushing scarlet. "I'm glad I got home early today. I've been wanting to meet all of you. I'm Sally Ryder."

"Oh . . . hello, yes. I'm sorry," Meg stammered.

"Heavens! Don't apologize. It was that old survival instinct doing its stuff, that's all. I've come in for my share of that kind of thing far too often not to recognize the

106

flinch of a fellow sufferer. Speaking of survival," she said, gazing out at the bedlam in the pool, "is everything under control out there, or should I be worrying?"

Meg sat up to see what was happening. "It's water polo," she explained. "Nobody's been drowned so far, but I'm glad I'm out here and not in there."

Sally laughed. "So am I."

There was such unmistakable warmth in the words that Meg suddenly felt comfortable and welcome, as if she and Sally were old friends. Before long she found herself talking freely and easily, telling Sally things she had needed to tell someone for a long time. Someone older, who would understand. When the time came for them to go, she was as reluctant to leave as Lew and Carey, and as anxious to come back.

14

As the days went by, Matt and the Schuylers gradually made themselves at home in each other's houses. The Schuylers had invented a game for Matt's benefit they called "People Practice." Matt never knew, when he rang their doorbell, whether one of them was going to answer the door, or whether it would be some make-believe character from the world he was about to reenter.

Once when the door opened, Lew was standing there in his father's trench coat. He had a moth-eaten hat balanced on his ears with a *Press Pass* stuck in the band, an unlighted cigarette butt sticking to his lower lip, and a pad and pencil in his hand—the classic reporter's get-up straight out of the late late movies. He had fired a series of questions at Matt designed to put him on the defensive or make him mad, but Matt had fielded them neatly and won applause from Will and Meg who were hiding behind the door.

Another time Will met him playing the suspicious father of a girl Matt was taking to the movies. He didn't do so well on that one, stumbling over his answers as he thought of Will's real father, whom he still had not met.

Mr. Schuyler had a positive aversion to his own house. Matt could understand that—too many memories waiting to jump him probably, every time he walked in the door. But since he worked late every night and organized all-day excursions for his family on Saturdays and Sundays, he was never in the house when Matt was. As far as Matt was concerned, the longer this went on, the better. Meg swore she could handle the introductions, but what father in his right mind was going to let his daughters have anything to do with a guy who might have killed one little girl already?

Meg played a succession of females, from the catty school gossip to a horrified teacher. She was his toughest inquisitor, backing him into verbal corners, bullying him into standing up for himself. "You've got rights too, Matt," she insisted. "Maybe people do have the right to think what they want, but you have the right to live."

Only Carey refused to play this game. Whenever Lew challenged her, she said she was no good at it; but she told Will once that she hated the way Matt looked when he was answering their questions. She was afraid if she made him look like that, she would cry.

The Schuylers in turn were happy to accept Matt's daily invitations to use the pool. While the others horsed around in the water, Meg spent the afternoons unwinding in Sally's understanding company from her demanding and impossible role as stand-in for the mother they all missed. When Matt teased her about their nonstop conversations, she retaliated by hinting that never in a million years would he guess what they were talking about. Lew and Michael, discovering a mutual fascination for board games, also spent long hours at the kitchen table, with Mrs. B acting as occasional umpire and peacemaker.

The last week before school started could have been a disaster. Mr. Schuyler took his family on their annual camping trip to Yosemite, and Matt would have been lost if Sally had not filled his days with last minute preparations. He had a complete physical so he could take part in the school athletic program; took and passed his driver's training and also his test for the license; went shopping for clothes with Sally and Michael; met Ryder and Tony for lunch and was ceremoniously presented with keys to both of the Ryders' cars; and abandoned the bicycle for his own footpower after making the heartening discovery that he could manage a decent eight miles without strain.

When he had time to consider the days ahead, he could not believe how much the last few weeks had changed his outlook. His situation hadn't changed. He was still wearing that mile-high label, and people were still going to steer clear of him or ask him accusing questions, but thanks to the Schuylers, he had answers for them now. And while they were asking themselves what kind of a guy he was, he was going to be out on that track showing them, running harder than he'd ever run before. Some days he actually found himself looking forward to the year ahead.

He was not the only one with mixed feelings. One morning at the stable, Don admitted that he hated school. Always had. Everything swept by him too fast; he felt as if he were missing important announcements, getting everywhere a little too late, never catching up. And he never had time to finish work he had started. Matt's promise of help with registration and homework did little to erase the two lines of worry that had etched themselves into Don's forehead, but he had better luck with Michael.

Because his birthday came in the second week of December, Michael had been too young for kindergarten a year ago. Now that he was almost six and entering school for the first time, he was old enough to worry about what was going to happen to him and expect the worst. He came into Matt's room after supper one night and lay on the bed with him, his small bare feet planted on the wall, his head resting heavily on Matt's stomach. After twenty minutes of silence, he suddenly spoke.

"What if she doesn't like me?"

Matt, listening drowsily to the radio, was lost. "What—? Who?"

"The teacher. What if she's mean?"

Matt considered the question. It took him back to a day when he had asked his mother the same thing. "I had a teacher in kindergarten who didn't like me much," he said. "But I survived. Anyway, when you've got as many people who do like you as you have, Michael, you don't have to worry about the dummies who don't." Matt grinned. Whose morale was he trying to boost, anyway?

Michael's feet walked up the paneled wall as far as the knothole and down again while he digested this idea. Then he rolled over and, chin in hand, gazed at Matt for a long time. "You're my best brother," he said suddenly. "Don't forget."

"I won't," Matt promised. "You're my best brother, too."

Michael giggled, digging his fingers into Matt's ribs. As they wrestled happily on the bed, Matt was wishing he could run interference for this sensitive little kid, intercept the hurts and bruises that were going to come his way when he left the safe protective circle of his family and began to make a place for himself in the world outside.

I wish I could guarantee you safe passage, Michael, he told his little brother silently, but I can't. Nobody can. You'll have to face life like everyone else and handle it your own way. I hope to God you do a better job of it than I have.

15

Meg and Will stopped by early Tuesday morning to pick Matt up. Mrs. B sent him off with hugs and a banquet in a brown bag for his lunch. Jenny and Sally added kisses, and Ryder shook his hand and wished him luck. Michael followed him out the front door and stood on the steps, watching wistfully as the Schuylers' car backed down the drive. Before the small figure was out of sight, Matt sent him a thumbs-up sign and an encouraging, "See you at four!"

To make up for time lost last spring, Matt had to carry a full seven period schedule. Between occasional worries about Michael, and his bumbling attempts to steer himself and Don through the vast confusion of the first day, he had little time to anticipate trouble, but his nerve ends were painfully sensitive to the stares and whispers. It didn't take him long to decide that if there's anything worse than having people talk about you when you don't know what they're saying, it's when you do.

Only two people confronted him with the murder, one

of them his biology teacher. Throughout their brief conversation Matt was so often reminded of Will's pompous and flustered imitations during their game of practicing people, that he had a hard time keeping a straight face.

The other one wasn't so funny. Surrounded by a small group of his cronies, a guy stopped Matt in the corridor and wanted to know how it felt to get away with murder.

I bet it took you a while to come up with that showstopper, Matt told him silently. Out loud he said, "I don't know."

"Come on, McKendrick, we know who you are. You're the guy we read about—the one who killed that little girl in the Palace Theater."

"I'm the guy you read about, but I didn't kill her or I wouldn't be here now. The police record shows I'm cleared."

"That's not what the papers said," the guy said belligerently. The confrontation obviously wasn't going the way he'd planned; he liked his victims squirming when he pinned them to the wall.

"The papers didn't have the whole story," Matt said evenly. He was following the Schuyler script, trying to ignore the pressure building inside. The days when he could let it go and settle arguments with his fists were gone for good. "They never do, do they?" he added and, figuring that was as good an exit line as he was going to get, left them standing.

By the time he met Will and Don for lunch, he was feeling more optimistic about his chances for survival. It had been a rough day, but not as bad as he'd expected.

With the worst behind him he could relax and look forward to his last period.

Seventh period P.E.—running. He had been waiting for it all day. This was where no one could touch him. No one was even going to see him for dust. Out on the track it was between him and the stopwatch. Nothing else mattered. *When you're up, you're up . . . !* The old cheer kept going through his mind as he dressed down and, jogging impatiently from one foot to the other, waited for the coach to call the roll.

His name wasn't on it, and he stepped forward when Dunstan asked if he had left anyone out. He was the only one. Ignoring him, the coach told the rest of the big class to spread out on the field and do a series of warm-up exercises. When they were alone, the coach looked him slowly up and down.

"I know all about you, McKendrick," he said, and it was obvious from the way he said it that he didn't like what he knew.

It had happened before; it would happen again. But it would never matter as much as it did now. "Coach, it was a mistake—the Palace Theater thing. I didn't do it. The police rec—"

"You didn't do it?" The coach snorted. "What I heard was they couldn't prove it either way. That's not the same thing, is it?"

"No, but—"

"Shut up, McKendrick, and listen to me. Listen to me good. P.E. is mandatory in this school, or I'd tell you to go to hell. Just looking at you makes me want to puke. But if I have to have you in my class, I don't have to like it, and I don't have to worry about whether you like it either. I'm going to have you begging for a transfer in a week. Now —get out there and get moving and hope for your sake you don't make too many mistakes!"

Come on, McKendrick. Don't just stand there with your mouth open. This isn't biology the guy wants to ruin for you—it's running. Fight for it, you jerk!

They hadn't practiced this one; there was no script for it, and he had no time to be diplomatic. "I want to run," he told the coach. "Nothing you can do is going to make me transfer out of this class, and nothing you can do will make me quit."

His rugged face flushed and perspiring, Dunstan looked as if he could have cheerfully beaten Matt to a pulp. "You want to run, do you?" he said softly, threateningly. "All right, kid, you're going to run. You're going to run twice as far as everyone else—do twice the warm-ups, twice the work. I'm going to run you right off your feet. And you'll do what I tell you and keep your lousy mouth shut, if you don't want to find yourself arguing the facts of your case in front of those thirty kids out there! Is that clear?"

It was. Too clear. The coach didn't know it, but he was holding all the aces. Today had proved that he could face one person at a time, even a man as hostile and threatening as Dunstan, and argue the facts and circumstances of Katie's death with them. But not a crowd. A mob. No way. Matt swallowed. "Yes," he muttered.

"Warm up," Dunstan said shortly, and left.

While the coach was outlining the requirements of cross-

116

country racing for people wanting to make the team, Matt did a quick series of exercises, Dunstan's final threat overshadowed by the knowledge that he hadn't let the coach stonewall him. He was free to run. No matter how hard Dunstan worked him, he could take it. He would pick up a lot from what Dunstan taught the others and work himself until he was the best runner on the team. The coach couldn't ignore that, no matter how much he hated him personally.

It was a good plan, guaranteed foolproof. Matt hung on to it until the class began running around the track. Starting off in the lead, after two laps he found himself trailing all but the most hopeless members of the group. With Dunstan yelling about his clenched fists and the angle of his body, the more he tried, the more he came apart. He was nothing like the best one in this motley assortment of runners. So much for seven straight years of conditioning. So much for the last four weeks. He just didn't have it.

How could he lose something that had been part of him for half his life? You can run better than this, McKendrick, he told himself furiously. You're doing it every morning—running hard, feeling great, just like you used to. What the hell is going on?

A whistle blew. "Everybody on the grass," the coach bellowed, "except McKendrick. You keep going."

He made it around the oval one more time. When he reached the group again, he found an inconspicuous place on the grass and, face burning, listened to Dunstan taking his performance apart. The worst of it was that the coach wasn't saying anything that wasn't true. He had heard the same criticisms many times, both of himself and of other kids new to the sport.

"All right, McKendrick, on your feet." Matt stood wearily. "Someone told me you had the makings of a real runner. Go around again, and this time show us some kick on that last curve. I want to see a strong finish."

Matt gave it all he had, but there was nothing to give. Pulse hammering, lungs heaving, he forced himself to keep putting one foot in front of the other, while Dunstan jogged up and down the center of the field keeping even with him and yelling instructions he couldn't carry out.

"Move it out, McKendrick! You look like a fifty-year-old out for his morning stumble around the block. Get some kind of rhythm in those legs. One-two-three-four— I said, move it!"

He felt himself beginning to favor his weaker leg, limping a little. Knock it off! he raged silently. You're getting through this without any feeble excuses. Back on the grass he tried to control his rasping breath, while Dunstan took his technique apart step by step and eventually had the whole class laughing.

When everyone began running again he dragged himself up and managed to complete the four circuits at a kind of stumbling shuffle. Lapped twice by the leaders, exhausted and humiliated, he followed the crowd into the locker room. The pelting shower restored him somewhat, but Dunstan stopped him on the way out and administered the final blow.

"You call yourself a runner?" he said sarcastically. "I wouldn't call what you were doing out there today anything but horseshit! What the hell was going on?"

Finding Dunstan's contempt harder to deal with than his anger, Matt forced himself to look the coach in the eye. "I don't know what was wrong. I wish I did." What *had* happened out there? After all his plans, all the training he'd put in, was that the best he could do? It wasn't good enough, not if he was going to prove he was something more than a guy who got away with murder. But how? What more could he do? What the hell *was* wrong . . . ?

Locked in painful conflict with himself, he collected his books and joined Will and Don at the bus stop. Having no seventh period classes, Meg had already gone home with the car. When Will asked for the second time how it had gone, Matt shrugged, avoiding his eye. "Okay, I guess," he said, knowing Will would take the hint and drop the subject.

The Montgomery Boulevard bus was so crowded and noisy that he did not become aware of the silence that had fallen over the three of them until they made the transfer and were on the long haul up Verde Canyon. The other two looked as discouraged and defeated as he felt. Rousing himself with an effort, he nudged Don. "What happened? You don't look so hot."

Don glanced at him, surprised. "I'm not—no," he stammered. "Nothing happened. It was okay."

Will came to his rescue. "We don't look so hot? We don't look so hot?" His grin widened. He began to laugh. "Well, if we don't look so hot it must be contagious because, man, you should see yourself!"

Matt felt himself emerging from his depression like a swimmer breaking the surface after too long under water. "You jerk!" he said, giving Will a friendly thump on the head to cover his embarrassment at being so easy to read, and they spent their last ten minutes howling over Will's description of the special agonies of a sophomore on the first wild day.

What happened this afternoon, Matt decided as he jogged downhill from the bus stop to the Ryders', was a freak accident. First day nerves, that's all it was. Tomorrow when he was more relaxed, he'd show Dunstan and the others what he could do, and the rest of the year would be a different story.

A gleeful shout interrupted his thoughts, and he looked up to see Michael racing toward him down the drive. Catching his little brother in mid-leap, Matt carried him into the house slung over his shoulder like a sack of oats, while Michael's excited voice, coming from somewhere around his lower back, told Matt in nonstop detail about his own day.

"—and there's two teachers and they both like me, and we have a really big climber in our yard. I can stand on the top no hands, and there's a boy the same size as me and he—"

Hearing the commotion, Jenny came flying down the hall. Clinging monkeylike to one of Matt's long legs, she rode him as far as the kitchen, where he dumped Michael into one chair and fell into another himself. Jenny was up on his lap at once, holding his face in her small hard hands to be sure of having his undivided attention.

"We made gingerbread men, and I made one for everybody all by myself, didn't I, Mrs. B?" Without waiting for Mrs. B's agreement, she darted on to the next thing, which was a trip to the shoe store with her mother. Then they had picked Michael up at school and had lunch "all the way downtown at Daddy's building!"

Seeing Sally's diplomatic hand at work in all this excitement, Matt felt a sudden longing to tell Sally about his own day and his humiliating performance on the track, but she was not at home. Out somewhere on a writing assignment, Mrs. B told him. His need to tell someone about the disastrous day was gradually buried under the avalanche of chatter and the warmth of Mrs. B's friendly kitchen, and by dinner time he was able to give Sally and Ryder an objective rundown of his first day that had them laughing appreciatively. Of track he said only that he hadn't done as well as he'd hoped, but he was working on it.

16

Work on it he did—like a madman. With no encouragement from Dunstan, he followed his old routines and training schedule from the previous year, which had been worked out with the help of a coach who had known him a long time. But September vanished and he was still running like a schizophrenic.

In his early morning runs he felt great—loose and easy, with plenty of stuff left for that final surging effort. At school he would start thinking about the P.E. class before lunch, reporting to the field with one of Mrs. B's feasts solidifying in his stomach. After a few days of this he began giving his lunches to Don, but he was still knotted-up inside.

All it took was the sound of the coach's voice. As if a machete were slashing at the strings that made everything work in rhythm, Matt could feel his muscles tense and begin fighting each other. Dunstan never said anything that wasn't true, but the more Matt drove himself to do better, the more opportunities he gave the coach to shoot him down.

Otherwise school was going pretty well. After the initial week or two of feeling he was a particularly nasty specimen under a microscope, he found the interest in him fading for lack of new fuel to feed it. The work itself wasn't much of a problem; but having grown up in a small community whose entire population was less than that of Lowell High, he was not used to people in such massive numbers. At the end of a gruelling day he sought out Will's and Don's uncritical company with relief and fell into the habit of taking his books to the public library three or four afternoons a week so he could study with Don and make good on his promise to help with his homework.

Don's biggest problem was reading. If he had something read to him, he could remember it, but it took him so long to decipher it himself that there wasn't enough time in a day for him to get all his assignments done.

Many times Matt thought of the hours his mom and dad had put in teaching Katie. If someone had spent half that time with Don when he first started school, he wouldn't be having so much trouble now. But Don wasn't a complainer, and Matt kept his occasional anger and frustration to himself. It was more usual, when he had been in Don's unhurried company for any length of time, for him to feel as jostled and threatened as Don did by the people around them who were rushing through life at breakneck speed. Small wonder Don was more comfortable with animals.

Sometimes Will came to the library with them. Matt suspected it was to get some relief from the never-ending demands Meg had to make on him to help her run the house; but Will wasn't a complainer either. All he would

say, with his usual grin, was that he needed the intellectual
stimulation.

Will was with Matt the night he found Cat.

The two of them were sitting at the bus stop in the
shopping center opposite Verde Canyon Road. Will was
describing a weird movie his sophomore English class had
seen that morning, when Matt held up his hand.

"Wait a second, Will. I hear something."

"What?"

"I'm not sure. Wait here. If the bus comes, yell."

Exploring the area behind the supermarket, he found a
tiny scrap of a kitten, almost too far gone to cry. Curled in
his hand it felt as fragile and bony as a baby bird. Tucking
the small survivor inside his shirt, Matt made it back to the
bench as the bus was pulling in.

Halfway up Verde Canyon, Will said something in a
voice so low, Matt had to ask him to repeat it. "I said,
that's how we got our three cats."

"Found them?"

"Rescued is more like it. All of them by my mom."

"That's a switch," Matt said, thinking of Poor Boy.
"Usually it's the kids who bring them home."

"She was full of switches like that. We used to kid her
about being a professional rescuer. Everyone from lost kids
in department stores to old people with flat tires on the
freeway. She always said she was a born busybody, but it was
really because she cared a lot about people, whether she
knew them or not, and she wasn't embarrassed to show it."
Will stopped abruptly, staring out the dark window at the
half-hidden lights along Verde Canyon.

Matt knew what he was thinking. If she hadn't cared so much about people, strangers included, they wouldn't have lost her. And they wouldn't be hurting so much now. It was a lousy deal, like Don said. Nothing he could say would make it better. He could listen, when Will wanted to talk about her, but that was all.

Some time passed before Will resumed the conversation. Matt had surreptitiously unbuttoned his shirt to make sure the kitten was still breathing and was stroking the tiny head with his forefinger.

"Do you think the Ryders will let you keep it?" Will asked.

"Let me keep—? Oh lord, I never thought of that." A thought struck him, and he grinned. "Sure they will. They kept me, didn't they?"

They did not disappoint him. Mrs. B rose to the occasion at once, and the kitten promptly found itself snuggled into a bed made of clean rags and a hot water bottle, its belly full of warm milk and oatmeal. By the time Sally and Ryder knew it was there, Michael had named it Mittens for its two white paws; and Jenny had donated her smallest stuffed animal—a shocking-pink hippo—to keep Mittens company.

Downplaying his own role in the rescue, Matt retired to the background and let Jenny and Michael do the persuading. Sally was concerned for the kitten's health. Ryder, catching Matt's eye, assumed an exaggerated air of martyrdom.

"Dogs, horses, cats—what next?" he asked the ceiling in mock despair, but in the end Mrs. B's assurance that she would be happy to feed it if Matt would take care of the shots and the housebreaking, tipped the vote in favor of Mittens' acceptance.

Later that night on his way to bed, Matt stopped briefly in the kitchen. "You don't know how lucky you are, cat," he told the sleeping kitten softly, thinking about his own fantastic luck. Tony, the Ryders, the Schuylers and Don—without them, *he* would not have survived.

A shiver ran through him. Luck can change. It had been a long time since he'd thought about the nightmare he had after going back to Craigie, and the fierce argument he had with himself afterwards. Running hadn't worked out the way he had wanted it to, but he'd been right about the way people would react to him. Had he been right or wrong about the idea that he could still do something that would make the Ryders change their minds about him?

There was no way to tell. He shoved the black thought into the back of his mind, determined not to let it surface again.

17

For a while after school started, Meg was so irritable and bossy that Matt was glad she was usually tied up in the afternoons. One crisp October day, though, she stayed through seventh period and offered him a ride home. He was trying to think of a tactful way to refuse when he recognized her expression as one he hadn't seen in weeks. Last summer's mischief-loving horseback rider was offering him this ride, and he accepted with alacrity.

"Nothing to do and nobody needing me for a whole afternoon!" she told him ecstatically. "I can't believe it!"

Like a switch, the words and the tone in which they were spoken threw a sudden light on her recent exasperating behavior. Housekeeping chores, appliance breakdowns, dentist appointments, shopping trips—no wonder she was such a pain. She was wearing herself out trying to be a full-time cook, chauffeur, and housekeeper as well as full-time student. "You want to go up to the stables?" he asked.

"Do I?" she said emphatically. "Let's go!"

Now that he knew what her problem was, he knew

better than to accuse her point-blank of trying to do too much. He had already tried to tell her a couple of times that her father should be sharing more of the load and had his head bitten off for his pains. "What more do you want him to do?" she had demanded, bristling at the idea that she couldn't handle everything herself. "He works all day. He's got his own worries. He can't come home and do the housework too."

Matt had also been present one morning when Will and Meg had blown up at each other over this same issue. Meg had wanted Will to take the Bachelor Living course so he could learn to cook something besides spaghetti, and Will was refusing because it would mess up his entire schedule for next semester. She had yelled at him to grow up and start carrying his share around the house; and he had told her fiercely that no one had asked her to be their mother and if she didn't like the job, everyone would be glad if she quit.

Stopping abruptly, they had stared at each other in mutual anguish, the silence heavy with things they wanted to tell each other and didn't know how, until Meg had turned and bolted from the room. Nothing more was said, but Matt noticed that Will, enlisting the help of Carey and Lew, had taken over a few more housekeeping chores like vacuuming and doing the dinner dishes.

They could use some help, and since he was practically a permanent fixture in their house he ought to be able to find some way to make himself useful. He came up with an idea at once, but he had to work out his approach carefully so Meg would think she was doing him a favor by accepting his offer. She was turning onto Las Lomas when he decided he was ready.

"You know something?" he said casually. "You really are lucky."

"Me? Why?"

"You've got a car and places to go. Do you know—since I got my license, I've driven Sally's car about ten times and Ryder's Mercedes exactly once?"

"Poor, poor baby boy," she drawled, oozing false sympathy. "I'd trade places with you any day."

That was exactly what he wanted her to say. Dropping the subject for the time being, he let the idea get a toe-hold, mentioning off-handedly on the way home that if she ever really wanted to trade places, he'd be glad to have an excuse to take somebody somewhere.

A few days went by before he realized she would never ask him. Too much like admitting she couldn't cope by herself. He had to say something like, "Anybody have to go anywhere tomorrow? I've got the car," before he would find himself a spectator at one of Lew's soccer league games or reading comic books in the orthodontist's office while Carey had her braces adjusted.

He was rewarded for his time one Saturday late in October when he offered to take Carey to a weekend swim meet so Meg and Will could accept an invitation to stay with friends in the mountains. When he picked Carey up at the crack of dawn, she climbed shyly into the back seat, and apart from giving him occasional directions said nothing at all during the forty-minute drive.

He had not been to a swim meet in a long time and had

vague recollections of endlessly repetitive heats of the same stroke swum by different age groups. Although Will had warned him and he had brought the thickest paperback in his collection, he was not prepared for the eighteen-page program that Carey brought up to their seats at the top of the bleachers.

He thought he had disguised his dismay, but after he'd asked her to show him what events she was in so he could watch, and she had silently pointed out the four places where her name appeared, she glanced at him shyly from under her dark lashes.

"I'm sorry you had to bring me," she said suddenly. "It was mean of Meg to make you come."

Before he could protest, she was leaping nimbly from row to row down toward the pool. When she materialized some time later at his side, she was wet and shivering and clearly upset.

"How did you do?" he said, hoping she wouldn't realize he had missed her event.

"Terrible!" she burst out. "I worsened my time by two whole seconds!" Rubbing furiously at her eyes, she fumbled in her bag. "Oh boy," she wailed. "What a day! I forgot the pencil. I'm never going to remember all my times."

Her voice was rising. Recognizing the signs, Matt hastily averted an explosion by producing a stubby pencil of his own. He sympathized with her disappointment. He went through the same experience in track, or used to anyway when his performance had been worth timing. "What's your best stroke?" he said, using Will's technique of distraction to calm her down.

"Freestyle," she said. "I'm only eight-tenths of a second off an "A" time in fifty Free."

"Is that good?"

"It's good for me. I've been swimming for almost a year, and I haven't gotten an "A" time yet."

"I know how you feel," he told her. "I've been running for seven years, and this year I'm so lousy the coach won't even let me on the team."

"He must be crazy!" Carey said hotly. "Will says you're the best runner he ever saw." Her conviction that he was the best warmed him considerably, even though he knew it came from Will's having said it and not from any knowledge of his skill.

Carey did much better in her 100-yard Individual Medley, proudly reporting a 2.4 second improvement. Her third event was the 50 Free. Matt watched the first three heats, wondering anxiously where she was, before he remembered to look in the program. She was swimming in the next-to-the-last heat, and once in position on the starting block she looked up toward the stands. He stood and gave her the thumbs-up sign.

The gun went off. The race began. Stroking smoothly and effortlessly down the pool, Carey slowly began to fall behind.

"Come on, Carey," Matt muttered. "Come on . . . you can do it."

She made her turn in a swirl of water and surfaced, swimming steadily but not hard enough. He knew it was not hard enough, and suddenly the outcome of this race became important to him too.

Forgetting his preference for remaining invisible in large crowds, Matt let out a yell. "Come on, Carey! Go for it!"

Whether she heard him or had planned it all along, with three-quarters of the pool remaining, she suddenly took off. "Go, Carey! Way to go, Care!" People around him were smiling as he cheered her on at the top of his voice. With both of them giving it everything they had, she pulled out a second place, and Matt felt as if he had swum the entire two lengths with her.

He reached the deck a moment later to find her surrounded by a group of excited friends. Bursting out of the crowd, she raced towards him shouting, "I did it! I did it!"

"Great going, Care!" he told her. "You were terrific!" Her smile was so wide, her eyes so brilliant, that looking at her made him feel terrific too.

After that triumph, her last race was an anti-climax. She had her "A" time medal and a fifth place ribbon for the 50 Free. Nothing else mattered. Riding home on the front seat beside Matt, she kept humming to herself and rubbing the medal to keep it shiny.

"I'm sorry Meg or Will wasn't here to see that performance," he told her at one point.

"I'm not," she said instantly. "I'm glad it was you. I wouldn't have gotten it without you."

"Could you hear me yelling?"

She grinned. "Once, but it wasn't that. I made a deal . . ." Her voice trailed off uncertainly.

"What kind of deal?" Matt could not quite picture the eleven-year-olds placing bets on each other's races.

"I promised if I got my "A" time, you'd get on the track team." She watched him anxiously for his reaction.

"Who'd you promise?" he said half-seriously. "I need to talk to them."

She thought this over. "I don't know," she said at last. "Maybe it was you."

Several times in the next few days, Matt thought about the burst of extra effort that had won Carey her "A" time. If that were all he needed, he'd be home free by now. But that was part of his trouble; he was putting everything he had into it already, trying too hard. Two-thirds of the cross-country season was behind him, and if anything he was worse than when he had started.

At last on a damp, chilly Thursday he discovered what was wrong. Dunstan wasn't coaching that afternoon. The varsity squad captain was filling in for him, and the guy treated Matt like just another member of the class. The tension that he usually brought with him to practice unknotted itself during the warm-up. Suddenly he had it all together again. Lapping the rest of the team a couple of times, he reveled in the disciplined freedom of his movements and the knowledge that it wasn't lost. It was there, when he wasn't in such a panic about Dunstan that he wound himself up to the breaking point.

"Why am I so scared of Dunstan?" he said on the way home on the bus that afternoon with Will. Will had just lost a close tennis match and was uncommunicative. Matt gave himself the answer. "Because he knows who I am."

Will roused himself. "So? What's to panic about that?"

"I mean he knows about the Palace Theater."

"So—? I thought we settled all that a long time ago."

Since that one time in the Schuylers' kitchen, Matt had not mentioned his private fear of crowds again. With Meg he didn't want to; she had problems of her own, and he never heard her whining about them. And with Will he didn't have to. Will was sensitive to other people's feelings and too private a person himself to go blundering around where he knew he wasn't wanted. His radar had picked a lousy time to go on the blink.

"So I keep waiting for him to get mad enough at me to tell the other thirty kids in the class about it," Matt said curtly.

Will stared. "Matt, you're kidding, aren't you? Tell me you're joking. Please?"

"Knock it off," Matt told him sharply. "I'm not in the mood for fun and games right now."

"Neither am I. Are you telling me that because Dunstan was blackmailing you about the Palace, you've been making a basket case of yourself and messing up the cross-country?"

"Will—!"

"Matt, most of those guys know who you are already. Who you really are, not Dunstan's version."

It was Matt's turn to stare. "What? How—?"

"I told them myself," Will said simply. "Whenever I heard someone passing along the wrong story, I'd give them the facts. You know—do them a favor and let them in on the inside story. I've only had two people, a couple of brainless girls, who liked Dunstan's version better."

Neither of them said another word until they got off the bus at Las Lomas and were standing at the side of the road. Staring into Matt's glazed eyes, Will pretended alarm. "Hey, Matt, are you okay? You look shell-shocked."

Matt felt shell-shocked. For once it was not such a bad

feeling. "Will Schuyler, so help me— I don't know whether to shove you down the storm drain or bronze you and put you up on a pedestal somewhere!"

Will sprinted across the road before Matt could make good either threat. "Get going, you nut!" he yelled out of the darkness. "And good luck!"

I'm going! I'm going! He was going to show the whole damned world he was a runner, but first he had to prove himself to his coach. "Hey, Will?"

Will's "What?" sounded faint and far away.

"Tell Carey I'm about to make good on the other half of her deal." An unintelligible question was shouted back. "Just tell her. She'll know what I mean. And tell her thanks."

18

Dunstan's hold could not be shaken off immediately, but by the first week of November, Matt knew he was coming out of it at last. He spent two weekends practicing runs over some cross-country courses the team had already run without him. One Sunday he took Will and Michael along—Will to time him, and Michael to cheer him on.

"It's not really accurate," he said of the result. "In a race there's a lot of jockeying around for places, which adds something to your time. But it's okay." It was more than okay. It was his lifetime best. He was on his way.

He said nothing to Dunstan the following Monday, knowing it would be a waste of breath to try to argue the coach into giving him a chance. He had to show the coach what he could do and leave the rest to him. Dunstan worked him unusually hard all that week, and Matt gloried in his ability to do anything the coach demanded after all the humiliating weeks of being the lousy example and the butt of all his jokes. He knew Dunstan was testing him to see how permanent this sudden improvement was.

The Wednesday before Thanksgiving a race was scheduled. Matt's name was not on the list posted on the bulletin board. "Hell," he said softly, reading the list again to make sure. That left only one race before the Championship, next week's run at Clairmont Park.

There was an unwritten rule about cross-country teams. Anyone could be on them who showed enough interest. He could have challenged his exclusion and taken his complaint to the head of the P.E. department, but he wasn't going to. He wanted Dunstan to recognize his ability and let him run in spite of what the man thought of him personally. He knew that if he could make Dunstan acknowledge that he was a runner, and a good one, he could prove it to the rest of the world.

For the three days of practice that followed Wednesday's race, Matt was in an agony of suspense. Each afternoon he hoped Dunstan would tell him he had made the team, but the closest the coach came to acknowledging Matt's improvement was the silence that had replaced the coach's former sarcastic appraisals of his technique.

On the last Thursday, he came to school prepared to run. The list did not go up all morning. Dunstan had it with him when the team assembled in the locker room that afternoon. As the coach read off the names and assigned everyone to cars for the ride out to Clairmont, Matt listened with head down so Dunstan could not see how desperately he was hoping to hear his name.

"That's it. Get moving."

The list was finished. His name was not on it. Stunned by the unfairness of it, he looked up to find Dunstan smiling broadly. Matt stood, track shoes dangling from his hand. "Coach," he said quietly, "I want to run this one."

"I've been waiting to hear you say that," Dunstan told him, "so I could have the satisfaction of giving you the answer. No."

"Why not?"

"You really want to know?"

"Yes."

"I'll tell you why not. You've been goofing off all season, playing some kind of fool game that you can't run worth a damn—"

"That's not—"

"—and now you've changed your mind and want to play with the big boys. I'm telling you—no go. As far as I'm concerned, you're still a lousy competitor, a bad sport, and a kid who's no asset to my team."

"Wait a min—"

Dunstan cut him off. "If you think I want the name McKendrick associated with Lowell after what you did— forget it. As long as I'm coaching here, McKendrick, you aren't running on any team."

Not running? Not on any team? Long after Dunstan left, Matt stood where he was, stunned by the impact of the coach's threat on his future. No running meant no chance to prove himself, no chance for an athletic scholarship at any university, no chance for his secret dream, a shot at the Olympics. . . .

No way. He wasn't quitting yet. Suddenly Matt exploded into action. Meg—he needed Meg! She had the car today. He raced toward the parking lot, furiously working out the details of his plan. If Dunstan could do without him, he could do without Dunstan, the bastard! He'd change into his Craigie colors—nothing in the rules said he couldn't run unattached—and get Ryder's stopwatch. He'd need Will to time him, too, in case Dunstan didn't, and— Jesus! Was there going to be enough time?

Meg was lounging against her car, talking with three of her friends. As Matt came roaring up, they scattered nervously.

"Sorry," he said. "Meg, listen, can you wait for me? I need a ride home."

"I thought you were running this afternoon."

"I am, but not with— Never mind, I'll tell you later. Can you wait while I get Will?"

"Yes, but hurry!" she yelled after him. "I have to take Carey to the orthodontist."

Matt ran. He found Will volleying with another sophomore and thanked his lucky stars there was no match today. "Hey, old buddy," he called through the fence, "I hate to do this to you, but I need your help."

Will jogged over. "What's up? Why aren't you—?"

"Tell you later. Can you come? Right now? Don't bother to change."

Will nodded, yelled to his partner that it was an emergency, and took off after Matt.

Meg's car being tied up for the afternoon threw Matt's plans off a little, but the discovery that Sally wasn't home was a real setback. After Meg dropped them off at the Ryders', they had about seven minutes before the next bus. Matt managed to change his clothes while tearing through

139

the house looking for Ryder's stopwatch; and Will raced up the hill to delay the bus if he could. The driver was one of the regulars who knew them, and he slowed up so Matt could leap on across from the Ryders' driveway. So far, so good.

Of the two transfers they had to make, the first one took only three minutes. Waiting at the second stop for a bus that was never going to come in time, Matt felt the pressure mounting unbearably. So much depended on this race. He *had* to make it. Clenched fists thrust deep into the pockets of his warm-up jacket, he prowled up and down the block like a caged panther. As he passed the bench for the fourth time, Will's sprawling figure suddenly came to life.

"The British are coming!" he shouted. Springing to his feet, he grabbed Matt's arm and gestured wildly back the way they had come. "The British are coming!"

Letting out a guffaw that blew most of his tension away, Matt glanced hastily around to see if anyone had noticed Will. Only about ten or fifteen people, that was all. Choking back his laughter, he punched Will a few times to shape him up. "Shut up, you clown!" he said in a fierce undertone. "What are you—crazy or something?"

Will's cringing posture and pleas for mercy were too convincing. A tottery old lady was glaring so fiercely at Matt, he was glad she wasn't carrying an umbrella.

"With friends like you," he muttered as they boarded the bus a moment later, "who needs enemies?"

"Sorry." Will's apology was contradicted by the glint of laughter in his eye. "Can't imagine what came over me."

"Next time you feel whatever it was coming on," Matt told him with feeling, "give me some warning so I can get a couple of miles away first."

"Some friend you are. One tiny lapse, one infinitesimal flaw, and you're ready to call it quits."

Not quits, Matt told him silently. I need you, friend. You and your crazy sense of humor, and your knack for making molehills out of mountains. I wish I could tell you that without its sounding corny, but I don't know how.

For the rest of the ride, he balanced on the edge of his seat, urging the bus on. He had to get there before the last race. It was his last chance to prove himself . . . to Dunstan, and then to the world.

19

The instant the doors swished open at Clairmont, Matt was out of the bus and heading at a run for the distant crowd. A race was about to start. By the time Will caught up, Matt was shedding his warm-up suit while he listened to an official's instructions about the race.

"It's the varsity race," Matt told him, his dark eyes glowing. "Wish me luck."

"Luck," Will panted, but Matt had gone. He spoke briefly to another official, who nodded and made a note at the bottom of his sheet. Will watched as Matt found a place in the line-up at the other end from the Lowell team and waited for the gun.

With the crack of the gun, Will punched the stopwatch and leaned wearily against a parked car as the pack of runners vanished over a distant rise. He was thinking how long it had been since he had first read about the beating-to-death and possible rape of a very small girl and the boy who'd been arrested at the scene. It seemed another lifetime.

The stories in the newspapers last spring had been so

contradictory, he had not known what to believe, but when he saw Matt at a couple of interscholastic track meets at the end of April, he took it for granted he had been cleared. The news that Matt had run and been found badly beaten in the canyon, and the lip-smacking rehash of the Palace murder in the papers, had not changed his mind. It had made him mad, though. It made him even madder now that he knew Matt. Why the hell, when you give them a choice, do people always choose to believe the worst about someone and not the best?

It was different with everyone who got to know Matt. None of the kids who knew him even slightly thought he could have killed his sister or anybody else. The whole situation—the whispers, the accusations, the coach's attitude—was so unfair! What really bugged him, and Meg too, was that Matt didn't think fair or not fair had anything to do with it. He saw it as a fact he had to live with, like being deaf or fat, or slow like Don. Something he couldn't change. Once people stick a label on you, it's hard to get it off.

But if he was slow to defend himself, Matt was quick to put himself on the line for someone else. That time with Boo, for instance. Or Don. All his life people had been writing Don off as a nothing, a nobody. By being Don's friend, Matt had made him feel like a somebody for a change. Not that Matt seemed to realize it. Any guy who can tell you that as a friend he's a definite liability and it's okay if you want him to get lost, obviously doesn't have the foggiest idea what kind of a guy he is. If Matt hadn't come along last summer when he did, the four of them would have been basket cases by—

143

"You a friend of McKendrick's?" A harsh voice brought Will back to the gray winter afternoon. Dunstan was standing in front of him, waiting for an answer.

Will did not appreciate the way the question had been put. Was this the guy the other kids kept telling him was such a great coach? Tough, yes . . . but fair too? It was hard to believe. "Yes," he said. "A good friend."

"What the hell does he think he's doing out there?"

Will knew Matt would not appreciate anyone messing in his private war with Dunstan. "Running," he said shortly.

"I told him he couldn't run. I don't want his name associated with Lowell. He's got a lousy rep—"

"Sir, wait a minute," Will interrupted recklessly. "He's got nothing to do with you or Lowell. He's wearing his Craigie colors and running unattached. You're going to wish he was running for you, though, because he's going to win this race. He's a good runner, maybe a great one; and if it's proof you want, just watch him today and see!"

The lead runners suddenly hove into view, loping downhill towards them single-file. Matt was leading the second group, and as he ran past Will shouted his elapsed time. "Go, Matt!" he yelled as Matt rounded the bend a hundred yards further along the dirt road.

Dunstan had left to clock Lowell's runners as they straggled past with the main bunch. Relieved to see he wasn't coming back, Will was furiously kicking himself for having opened his big mouth. After all that, what if Matt didn't win? He began sending out one urgent message after another. *Come on, Matt . . . win it!*

144

It seemed forever before the shout went up as the first runner came back around the final curve. It was a blond kid in dark navy trunks. Right behind him was a wiry black guy. A couple of paces behind him, and coming up fast, was Matt.

"Go, Matt! GO!" Will yelled, trying to hold the hand with the precious stopwatch in it steady while the rest of him was going berserk. Matt came up the long tunnel between the two lines of curious officials and gawking spectators like a man running an Indian gauntlet for survival in the old West. "GO! GO! GO!" Will screamed, and Matt—his speed increasing with every stride—crossed the finish line 4.7 seconds ahead of his competition.

Will broke out of the line and raced after him, knowing Matt had kept going not only to prevent his muscles from tying up but to get as far as possible from the crowd. They were thumping each other on the back, gabbling incoherently, when Matt looked over Will's shoulder and froze. The blood drained out of his face. Will turned. A mob was advancing on them.

"Let's go," Matt said desperately. Too late. The curious crowd had surrounded them, and a puzzled official was elbowing his way toward Matt. The man raised his voice above the hubbub.

"Your name is McKendrick?"

A muscle along Matt's jaw swelled and vanished. "Yes, sir."

"I understand you were running unattached." The man had to tilt his head back slightly to look up at Matt.

"Yes."

"How old are you?"

"Sixteen."

Oh lord, Will thought in sudden panic. They think he's a ringer from one of the colleges. With his height and build, and the strained watchful expression on his face, he looked a lot older than sixteen.

"Can you prove that?"

Matt reached automatically for his back pocket, flung a desperate glance at Will, and shrugged. "I don't have my wallet or my license with me—no, sir."

The red-faced official was convinced that Matt was pulling his leg. "This is a high school race. I'll have no choice but to disqualify you if no one can vouch for your age, you know."

Will could not stand by and let this happen, not after Matt's great win. "I can," he said loudly.

"I bet you can," the official said with heavy sarcasm.

"I can, sir. And so can his coach."

"Forget it, Will." Matt's tone was flat and uncompromising.

"Tell them who he is, Matt. It's your race. You won—"

"No."

Will had said enough for one day. Taking a deep breath, he shut his mouth before the rest of the angry words came boiling out.

"What school do you go to?" the official persisted, giving Matt one more chance.

"Forget it," Matt said curtly. "Disqualify me. It doesn't matter."

"It does matter. The first five runners in this race go on to the City Championships next week."

The Championships? Matt went very still. He stared at the man for a moment and then, as if he had made up his mind about something, slowly began searching the faces around him for his coach. He found Dunstan at the edge of the crowd. Their eyes met.

Come on, Dunstan, Will said under his breath. Come on! He's earned this win. Think what you want to about the Palace, but let him have this one.

Giving a slight, almost imperceptible shake of his head, Dunstan turned his back on Matt and strode rapidly across the field toward his car, disowning him.

You bastard! Will screamed after him silently. You rotten bastard . . . !

Matt drew in a long, shaky breath. "I'm sorry," he told the waiting official. "If I can't run unattached, I can't run."

"I'm sorry too, son." The man seemed less hostile now that the issue was settled. "You ran a beautiful race."

"Thanks," Matt said bitterly. "Let's go, Will."

On the long trek home, Will maneuvered both of them on and off the commuter-jammed buses and paid their fares. Matt had shut himself away in some inner place, remote and unreachable. The fist in his lap kept clenching and unclenching. Will remained silent, too. One look at Matt's drawn face had shown him what Carey meant when she refused to play the "people" game. When they reached Las Lomas and Matt managed a crooked smile and a "Thanks, friend," Will headed for home at a run. He didn't want Matt to see him crying either.

20

Friday afternoon Matt turned up at practice as if nothing had happened the day before. It had taken him most of the night, but he had argued himself into hanging on and making Dunstan acknowledge him if it took until the end of the year. The rest of the class, having heard about the race and its aftermath, was unusually subdued. None of the kids actually said anything, but there was an edge to the way they congratulated him on a great race that told Matt they thought he had gotten a raw deal. It made him feel he had proved himself to them at least. You're next, Dunstan, he told the coach silently on the way out of the locker room. You can't hold out forever.

Meg and Don were waiting for him outside the door.

"Matt, something awful's happened," Meg began, but Don interrupted her, something he never did.

"Matt, I need you to help."

"What?" Matt said sharply, looking from one to the other. "What's wrong?"

"I heard Aunt Cora and her boyfriend. As soon as I'm

eighteen, they're going to com—commit me to an institution."

"Going to what?"

"Commit me. To a mental retard institution."

After what he had been through with Katie, the word
institution hit Matt in an unprotected place. "The hell
they are!" he burst out. "You're not retarded. How can
they do that?"

"It's not Aunt Cora's idea," Don said, as if that mattered. "It's Arnie's."

"Once Don is eighteen, she won't be getting any more
money from Foster Parents," Meg said bitterly. "They
just want to get rid of him, that's all."

"But how can you send somebody to an institution like
that without any—? When's your birthday?"

"The twelfth," Don said miserably.

"A week from Sunday," Meg added.

"But I don't— An institution!" Matt made a helpless
gesture with his fist. "You know something? It's a lousy
deal sometimes, being a kid."

"So what else is new?" Meg said crisply. "Let's go up to
the stable. We need time to think."

They sat on the pine shavings in Cricket's stall and
watched the gelding slobbering enthusiastically over his
alfalfa meal while they talked in low voices.

"What if Don disappears?" Matt suggested. It had not
worked for him and Katie, but Don—

"You mean we find an abandoned shack," Meg said incredulously, "and bring him food for the rest of his life?
Matt, honestly!"

149

"I need to get a job," Don said. "I have to be able to take care of myself."

"Okay, okay," Matt said, relieved that no one had taken him up on his idea. "There must be a lot of jobs you'd be good at, Don. Anything to do with animals."

"What about a job right here with Mr. Santini?" Meg added.

"He's got Caesar and Miguel living here already," Don said. "He doesn't have anything except exercising like I've been doing. But that doesn't pay me enough to eat and live somewhere, too. I figured it out—what I need." He pulled a much-folded piece of notebook paper out of his pocket. Covered with his large scrawling print, it was a very thorough job, and it proved as he said that a job paying him two dollars an hour part-time wasn't going to do it. "Anyway," Don went on, "I want to finish high school, so I can't work full time until January. I've been thinking about it for two weeks, and I keep coming to a dead end. That's why I had to ask you."

They were silent for a while. Then Meg stirred. "Well," she said briskly, "now that you've done all the preliminary work, it shouldn't be hard for the three of us to find something, right?" But Matt knew she was wishing, as he was, that life would quit clobbering this gentle guy and give him a chance to go his own way at his own pace. He'd already been driven out of the flock because he was different. Why couldn't people let him be? One thing was certain. They were going to get him that job if they had to go to Pasadena to find it.

Meg had to take Carey to a swim meet the next morning, but Matt met Don at the stables. They went through the *Times* want-ad section together and were thoroughly discouraged by the time they were through. Not a single job listed had requirements that matched Don's limited experience and training.

Looking for a diversion, Matt took Don with him that afternoon to buy a present for Michael, whose birthday was the day before Don's. Since Michael was anxious to tell time the "real way," they decided on a multi-colored wristwatch that was supposed to make it easier for its wearer to learn.

"Don't worry, Don," Matt told him as they parted company. "On Sunday, with Meg running the show, we'll find something."

On Sunday they discovered how big a job they had ahead of them. Meg met them at the barn and suggested they try some other stables. Matt and Don exchanged, "See, what did I tell you?" glances and teased Meg by refusing to explain why, but their high spirits evaporated as the day wore on. Because Don stammered a lot when he was talking to strangers on the phone, they spent most of the day driving around talking to stable owners in person. No one was hiring on a full-time basis.

It was nearly dinnertime when they dropped Don off at his corner. Halfway up Verde Canyon Road, Meg abandoned her pretense of cheery optimism and revealed her lack of confidence to Matt.

"It's going to take a while," she said gloomily. "There's a job out there somewhere, Matt. There has to be. But we have only seven more days to find it, and that's not going to be enough time."

"Yes it is," he contradicted her roughly. He wasn't used

to hearing Meg admit defeat or uncertainty. It undermined his conviction that they were going to succeed. "If it's not, we'll just find him a place to stay while we're looking, that's all."

"Yes, sir, Captain sir!" Meg saluted him smartly. "I'll get on that right away, sir."

Matt thought he might have a solution to that problem himself. "I have an idea," he told her as he got out of the car. "I'll let you know in the morning if it works out."

"Well, I've got one too," Meg told him in a perfect imitation of Carey's "So ha-ha on you" voice. They both laughed, feeling better. "I'll pick you up tomorrow at the usual time."

Matt went slowly into the house. He needed time to work out the details before he put his plan into action, but it turned out he had more time than he wanted. A maniac with a knife was terrorizing the old and the derelict in the city. Although Matt waited up until after midnight, Ryder never came in that night at all.

They tried out Meg's idea during fourth period on Monday—the three of them going to the school's Career Center to ask the woman in charge for advice. She was cordial enough to begin with, but after she had listened for a few minutes to Don's halting attempts to explain what he was good at, she became nervous and short with them. Avoiding their eyes, she told them to come back in a week or so. In the meantime she would see what she could do.

"Thank you anyway, but don't bother," Meg said rudely. "A week or so will be too late."

"Meg—" Matt said warningly. On Sunday they had

agreed not to let Don see how worried they were about the difficulties ahead of them. She vanished into a convenient restroom, and when she reemerged she had herself under control.

"Matt, can you cut seventh period today?" she asked. "We can hit about six stables in the Valley if we get an early enough start."

"No problem," he said. His feud with Dunstan could wait. "I'll see you guys at two-fifteen."

It was another frustrating day. Late that afternoon, as Meg stopped in the Ryders' drive to let Matt out, he told her his plan. He was going to ask the Ryders if Don could stay with them until he found a permanent place.

"Do you really think they would?"

Meg sounded so hopeful that Matt felt suddenly encouraged too. "I don't know. I'm pretty sure if I wanted to have a friend down for a week, they'd let me." As Gary's freckled face flashed briefly through his mind, he destroyed the image instantly. "This isn't much different."

"Let me know as soon as you find out, okay?"

"I might," Matt said airily. "Then again, I might not. It depends." Meg tried to punch him, but he was out of the car and laughing while she was still tangled in her seat belt. "See you around," he said, slamming the door and taking the front steps in a single bound.

His good mood lasted until in answer to his question, Sally said she didn't know when Les would be home, or whether he was coming home at all, and was there anything she could do?

"I guess not, thanks." On something this important, he

thought the lieutenant would have to decide. If he asked Sally's permission first, Ryder might think he was trying to get her to plead his cause for him.

The door to the garage finally opened and shut sometime after ten that night, and it was all Matt could do to let the lieutenant relax and unwind a little before he disturbed him. Lying on his bed with the sleeping Cat a warm weight on his stomach, he imagined the coming conversation over and over in his mind. At last, unable to stand the suspense any longer, he went quietly down the long hall to the library. He was nervous about this conversation. The timing was bad. It would have been better at dinner when he and Ryder had already been talking for a while about other things, kidding around with each other the way they usually did, loose and easy.

Ryder was alone, slumped in his big leather chair. A half-empty glass rested on the table beside him and a forgotten cigarette was burning itself out in the ashtray.

"Sir?" Matt said quietly.

Ryder roused himself with difficulty. "Can it wait, Matt?"

Matt hesitated. Could it? "No . . . I'm sorry."

"All right, then. Shoot."

Ryder's use of Tony Prado's favorite phrase was a good omen. Matt plunged right in. "I have a friend who's going to be eighteen in a week. His foster mother won't be getting paid for him anymore, but she thinks he can't take care of himself, so she's going to have him committed to an institution."

"Why can't he take care of himself?"

"He's . . . slow at things like math and reading, but—"

"Is he retarded?"

"No! Not in anything that matters."

Ryder smiled. "And you want to do battle for him. Matt, I hate to have to tell you this, but there's nothing you can do."

"But he just needs to find a job and support himself. He can do it."

Irritation gave Ryder's voice a slight edge. "Are you asking me to give him a job?"

"No. His birthday is next Sunday, though, and we don't have much time to help him find one. I was wondering if you could let him stay here for a week or two, just until—"

"Stay here?"

"We could put the bunk bed back in my room and—"

"No, Matt."

"Sir, it would just be for a little while."

"Can you promise me that? Can you be absolutely certain that this slow kid is going to find a job in the next two weeks and be able to support himself for the rest of his life?"

"No, I can't," Matt said hotly, "but I don't think that's a fair question."

Ryder eyed him thoughtfully. "You're right," he said finally. "It isn't. What I'm trying to do is point out the potential problems with this arrangement. I'm sorry, Matt. It's not possible."

Matt knew the discussion was over, but he gave it one more try. "If it was just for a week—?" he had intended to say that no matter how things turned out, they'd arrange for Don to go somewhere else after that.

Before he could finish the sentence, Ryder exploded. "For Christ's sake, Matt, there are thousands of people in trouble in this city! You don't expect me to take in every one of them, do you? If this friend of yours can make it on his own, he will. If he can't, he'll be happier in an institution." Matt did not answer. Ryder leaned back in the chair and closed his eyes. "I'm sorry, Matt. Shouldn't be shouting at you. Too much work and too little sleep the last few days. . . ."

Matt barely heard this apology. Mouth frozen around a half-formed sound, he stood paralyzed, seeing not the powerful police detective but a tired, generous man who had taken in a kid in trouble and given him everything he needed. Not because he had to, like a parent, but because he wanted to. He could stop wanting to. . . .

What's wrong with you, McKendrick? This is your good buddy you're arguing about, not some stupid dog. Fight for him, for chrissakes!

I can't. The truth scorched Matt's skin and twisted so sharply in his stomach, he thought he was going to be sick.

You can't? Why not? Because you've gotten settled in here? Because you've been thinking of this place as home for a long time, and now you're scared of losing it? You coward! You stinking coward! You're scared to fight it out with him the way you would if he was your father. You're scared to find out what he'll do if you make him mad enough. McKendrick, you gutless—! You know what you're doing, don't you? You're saving your own lousy skin at Don's expense. That's the kind of terrific guy you are!

Choking back tears of shame and fury, Matt slammed the front door behind him a moment later and sprinted all

the way to Meg's. He rang the bell like a stranger, not using his special ring.

Will answered it. "What are you doing out here?" he
said, surprised. "Just come on in like you—"

"Tell Meg to come out here."

Without another word, Will went to get her out of bed.

Meg came out and closed the door behind her. They
stood on the front step under the light, looking at each
other.

"It didn't work, did it?" she said softly.

"No." He needed something solid to hang on to and
reached for her, a hand gripping each shoulder. "Meg," he
burst out, "I blew it! I really loused it up for Don, and
you want to know why? You want to know what I did?"
She nodded, intent on his face. "Ryder wanted to know
what would happen if he took Don in and Don never did
find a job. I guess he was thinking he'd be stuck with Don
forever, and I was trying to think of a way we could promise
him that wouldn't happen, only when I started to argue he
got mad. Meg, if Ryder were my own father, stuck with
me for better or worse, I would have gotten mad myself.
I would have yelled and bargained and said all the things
you only half mean when you're mad at your parents for
not understanding why something's important. Only he's
not my father. . . ."

"Oh, Matt—"

"Yeah. I folded up. I just stood there as if he'd laid me
out cold. I wasn't thinking about Don anymore. Oh no. I
was thinking about me—where I'd go if I made him so
mad he decided to throw me back where I came from."

"Matt, he wouldn't!"

"He could." *Go on, Meg, tell me he can't. Tell me I'm crazy and nothing's going to happen if I go back there and fight for Don.*

Her eyes never left his face. Suddenly they filled with tears.

I know, he told her silently. *That's what I thought too. Oh God . . . I'm sorry!* Desperate and furious, sick with shame—he whirled and left her at a run.

21

Matt suffered through Tuesday's classes with barely concealed impatience, taking few notes and bringing himself to the scathing attention of the biology teacher. He forgot it all as soon as he met Meg and Don in the parking lot after sixth period. Meg was in a foul mood, too. Matt fought with her several times over minor issues and bawled her out for making a last-minute lane change to get off the freeway, but it didn't get rid of the pressure building inside his chest.

When Meg finally dropped him off, it was after nine. He was so strung up he could hardly eat the food Mrs. B had saved for him and was beyond noticing the anxious way she watched as he picked at his meal.

Both Sally and Ryder were out late that night, and Matt left the house without breakfast on Wednesday morning to avoid seeing either of them. He and Meg and Don cut all their classes that day, trying their luck at two animal farms and four stables. Matt refused to believe there were no jobs. There had to be something. Don wasn't going to any lousy institution.

Don said less and less as the day wore on. "It's no use, is it?" he said heavily as they let him off at his corner late that night.

Matt turned on him fiercely. "Don't say that! Tomorrow we'll try the zoo and some other places in the city."

"I can't cut classes tomorrow," Meg objected. "I've got two tests and an experiment due Friday, and somebody has to take Carey to the orthodontist."

"We don't need you," Matt said, too wound up to realize how it sounded. "We can take the bus."

Twenty minutes later Meg let him off in his driveway and went home without another word. Matt went straight to his room and closed the door so no one would bother him. When Mrs. B knocked, he told her he had eaten a hamburger downtown.

He was deliberately cutting himself off from the rest of the Ryder household. Until he found Don a place of his own, he would not let himself feel at home here again. He and Don were in the same boat—both of them without families, both unacceptable in some way to the rest of the world. Either both of them got lucky, or neither one did. One of them wasn't going to get the breaks without the other.

He left the house so early the next morning that he had to wait for an hour in the shopping center coffee shop before Don showed up. They started off with a hunch that today would be the day, but drew blanks at the zoo and the aquarium. The jobs available for eighteen-year-olds either didn't pay enough for Don to live on, or required skills and training he didn't have. He could not even drive a car.

Over hamburgers and Cokes at lunch, Don fixed Matt with his disconcertingly steady gaze. "Matt, listen," he said seriously. Matt stopped chewing and waited. "I've been thinking a lot this week. I'm sorry I made so much trouble for you and Meg, but I want to stay around Lowell. I want a job where I know people. Out there—" He made a gesture that seemed to take in the world itself.

Matt heard the uncertainty in his voice and understood it. Don did not want to try to make it among strangers, completely alone. "Okay, Don, I know what you mean," he said gruffly. "Let's start walking in circles on the streets around Lowell. We can look for Help Wanted signs."

For the rest of the day they walked. Matt kept pulling himself up sharply, telling himself it was a job for Don they wanted. The search, and the turmoil inside him, were too reminiscent of his experience last spring. No one was going to commit Don to any lousy institution. That was settled. If it came down to the wire and there were no jobs in L.A., he and Don would take off together. They could take care of themselves; no one would waste time looking for them. He had been thinking about the possibility all week, but last night's nightmare had made up his mind.

He'd dreamed he was floating precariously on a tiny life raft after a shipwreck, surrounded by screams, explosions, circling sharks—the whole bit. When Don swam out of the darkness and tried to get on it with him, the raft began to sink. And he—Don's good buddy—had smashed at his fingers until Don let go and disappeared in a swirl of fins and blood and foaming water. *McKendrick, you—!*

"Matt?" Don's anxious voice broke through to him.

They were standing on his corner. "Listen, thanks a lot. I'll see you tomorrow."

"Yeah, sure. Okay," Matt said automatically, his mind still on the dream. "Don't worry, Don. We'll find something now we know where to look."

He was so preoccupied with plans for the day after Sunday that he let himself into the Ryders' without remembering to be quiet. As he shut the front door, Ryder called to him from the library.

"Matt? Would you come in here, please? I'd like to talk to you."

"What about?" Matt said curtly, determined to keep the lieutenant at a distance. He was burning his bridges so there would be nothing to hold him back if he had to leave. The lieutenant studied him for a moment in silence. You heard me right, Matt told him silently. Get mad. Yell at me. Make me hate you. Please. . . .

"Matt, Mrs. B tells me you haven't been home for supper all week, and she's had calls from the high school two days in a row asking where you are." Ryder paused. When Matt volunteered nothing, he rapped out sharply, "Where are you?"

What could he say? This was his problem now; nothing Ryder could do about it. Trying to avoid a direct answer, he said, "I won't cut classes tomorrow."

"Is that all you're going to tell me?"

"I'll apologize to Mrs. B."

"That isn't what I—" Ryder broke off abruptly. After a moment he said gently, "Can I help, Matt?"

The concern in his voice nearly destroyed Matt's resolve.

Sir, don't do this to me. Get mad or something, but don't . . . don't— "No," he said flatly, not trusting himself to say more.

Ryder sighed. "Good night, then."

"Good night." *And good-bye. And thanks.*

Oh Jesus . . . I don't want to go.

22

Friday went by in a meaningless haze. His mind a thousand miles away, searching out possible destinations for himself and Don, Matt turned up automatically for P.E. in the afternoon. He did not remember that for the last four days he had cut seventh period until Dunstan barked at him to wait in the locker room while the class ran out on the field.

When the last guy had left, Dunstan closed and locked the door. As the coach came toward him, flexing his big hands, Matt stood up slowly. His breathing harsh and rapid, his eyes glittering—Dunstan looked like a man about to commit murder. "Open your locker, McKendrick."

If he asked why, the coach would probably ram his teeth down his throat. Matt stood silently by, while Dunstan went through the pockets of his street clothes, throwing each thing on the floor as he finished with it. He was obviously looking for something. He was almost through when Matt decided to take a chance. "Coach—?"

"Shut up! When I want to hear from you, you little

punk, I'll let you know. Get this stuff picked up and get dressed."

Dunstan watched closely while Matt changed. When he started to put his track gear back in the locker, the coach stopped him. "Take that stuff with you, kid. You're through. I don't want to see you back here again."

There was no point in arguing; after Sunday he wasn't planning on coming back anyway. But now he had started burning bridges, there was no point in playing it safe either. "Why?" he said. "I can explain about the cuts this week."

"I'll bet you can. What happened? Your supplier run out on you?"

"My what?"

"Upstairs," Dunstan said harshly, shoving Matt ahead of him with a painful hold on the back of his neck. "Where's your book locker?"

"Down there—M one-twenty-five." They were in the upper hall, and a few kids were watching curiously. "Sir, I don't understand."

Ignoring the question, Dunstan tightened his grip. "Open it," he said roughly when they reached the locker. Taking out every one of Matt's books, he peered along the spines and riffled through the pages. When that was done he went over the inside of the locker as well.

Matt hazarded a guess. "I haven't stolen anything, if that's—"

"I'm looking for pills."

"Pills?" Matt echoed blankly.

"Yeah, pills. Anything you could have taken last Thursday to help you put out the way you did."

Matt's mind shut itself off completely for a couple of

seconds before it came on again at lightning speed. Dunstan thought he was taking drugs so he could run better. There was no way he could prove he wasn't. It was the Palace all over again. No evidence. No proof. Just his word—take it or leave it. And it had to happen today, of all days, when they couldn't afford the time.

Now what? He could deny Dunstan's charge—deny it to Dunstan, and if he didn't believe it, then to the principal, and then to the police, and eventually to Ryder. In the end he would have to tell them the whole thing—how and why he had messed up the cross-country season and what he had been doing for the past week.

Wait a second . . . what would happen when the police found out about Don's situation? Would they get into the act, take Don off his foster mother's hands? Put him away in an institution themselves? No way!

What if he took a chance on Dunstan now? Told him the truth about the cross-country and what a gutless coward he was. What did he have to lose? Compared to Don, nothing. Only his pride, and that wouldn't be worth a damn if he let Don down again.

"Coach," he said slowly, "I don't take drugs. If you'll give me a chance to tell you what happened—not make any more accusations until I'm finished—I think I can explain the whole thing."

Dunstan's face was no longer flushed, and he seemed calmer. He might be ready to listen. Will had changed people's minds by telling them the facts. If the coach was as fair as the other guys said he was, maybe—

The coach shrugged impatiently. "Okay, McKendrick, I'll give you five minutes. In my office."

Once inside the small room, which was dominated by trophies and photographs from past seasons, Dunstan propped himself on the edge of his desk while Matt remained standing.

"Go ahead," Dunstan said.

"It might take longer than five minutes."

"All right, I'm listening. Get on with it."

"Last April," Matt began, because he had to begin somewhere if he was going to get it over with, "my little sister was killed by someone in the Palace Theater while I was out looking for a job. We . . . we came from Idaho. Our parents died and they wanted to put Katie away. She was deaf." He was telling this all wrong, going backwards. Taking a deep breath, he pretended he was telling a story that happened to someone else.

"Homicide and Lieutenant Ryder thought at first I had killed her myself. Everyone did." Matt looked at Dunstan. The coach was watching him intently. "Coach, I don't want to tell you all this. I mean I'm not making excuses. I have to tell you because I—because it's why I made such a mess of the cross-country." Dunstan nodded briefly, and Matt went on.

"Something happened. I don't remember exactly, and Lieutenant Ryder never could find out, but there was a crowd of people. They thought I'd killed Katie. I couldn't make them believe me. Afterwards I had a broken leg and . . . and some other things. Ryder took me home from the hospital with him and I've lived with his family ever since. He believes me. There isn't any proof, though—like you said."

Matt took another deep breath. This was going to be

167

the hardest part. "Running is important to me. I've been working on it for seven years. I spent the summer in that cast, and when I came to Lowell I was nervous about my leg but I was ready to start running again. That first day, when you said you knew who I was, I didn't know why at first, but I was scared." It was out. The worst was over. He raced to finish it up. "All the time I was running so tightened up and everything, I was just scared."

"Of me?"

"Not of you exactly. You never said anything about my running that wasn't true. I didn't understand it myself for a long time, but I was scared I was going to have to face all those guys at once and try to explain about Katie. I was afraid I couldn't make a crowd believe me. It . . . it didn't work before."

"Christ!" Dunstan exploded. What had he been doing to this kid?

"I'm almost through," Matt said quickly. "I didn't figure out what was wrong until a couple of weeks before the Clairmont race. After that I started getting it together."

Dunstan grunted, remembering the time when Matt was getting it together. Remembering, too, his grudging admiration for the kid's tenacity and determination, his growing respect for McKendrick's toughness and courage. This kid was a hell of a good runner, the best he'd seen in all his years of coaching, and for the last week he'd been going crazy thinking McKendrick was throwing it all away on drugs. He'd almost killed him today . . .

"The Clairmont race wasn't a fluke," Matt went on, wondering if Dunstan was still listening. "I know I can run like that when I'm not scaring myself half-blind. And

168

I don't need drugs to do it, either," he added, remembering how all this had gotten started.

"You through?"

Matt nodded. In more way than one, he was thinking.

"How come you cut all this week, then, when you could have been showing me that race was no fluke?"

"A friend of mine needs to find a job by Sunday. Otherwise he'll spend the rest of his life in an institution for mental retards."

"That the big kid I've seen hanging around after practice?"

"Yes."

For a long time Dunstan appeared to be reading the autographs on a baseball he had been rolling around in his hand while Matt was talking. A muscle in his cheek bulged once or twice. He glanced up finally, and Matt stiffened.

"Seventh period is about over," Dunstan said gruffly. "That kid going to be waiting for you today?"

"Yes."

"You'd better get going then." Matt hesitated, not sure what this meant. "Beat it," the coach said again. "And McKendrick—" Matt paused, his hand on the doorknob. "I've been wrong about you twice, with a hell of a lot of help from you both times. Pull a stunt like that on me again"—was Dunstan actually grinning at him?—"and I'll break *both* your legs!"

Grabbing an assortment of books out of his locker, Matt raced to the parking lot. He wasn't sure which he wanted to do most, laugh or cry. This could have been one of the great days of his life. He was in! He had earned the right to run, and on top of that Dunstan believed him! The thing he'd been sweating over for the last three months had finally happened—just in time to be thrown away along with everything else he cared about. On Monday, when the coach found out he'd been wrong about Matt for the last time, he wasn't going to be half as sorry as Matt was.

Meg and Don were sitting in the car. He could see the unscheduled wait for him hadn't done either of them any good.

"What took you so long?" Meg demanded.

"Talking to Dunstan," he said shortly. Any other time it would have been cause for celebration, but now he didn't want to talk about it. The way he was feeling, he'd probably break down and bawl. "Where to today?"

Meg did not answer. He glanced up to find her staring at him in disbelief. "What's wrong?" he said irritably.

"You've got to be kidding," she said incredulously. "You know we've only got two days left. You keep us waiting for an hour that we could have been out doing something important while you chat with Dunstan, and you want to know what's wrong?"

Matt drew his breath in sharply. That *something important* really got to him. "Did anyone ever tell you," he said bitterly, "that you can be a real witch?"

"Lots of times," she shot back at him, but she was blushing.

Scratch one more friend, he thought. Good at that, aren't you, McKendrick? A lot better than you are at keeping them. "Let's go—wherever we're going," he said shortly. Meg silently maneuvered the car out onto the crowded streets.

They drove until long after dark, stopping to investigate three Help Wanted signs and an assortment of large and small grocery stores without results. Meg finally suggested they go up to the stable and talk about the next step. The trouble was that once they were settled in Cricket's stall, scene of last Friday's optimistic plans, no one had any fresh ideas. All they could get out of Don was the increasingly desperate assertion that he had to be able to support himself.

"Look, Don," Meg said impatiently, after he had repeated this for the third time. "You're going to find a job. You need more time, that's all. Maybe that's what we should be thinking about—where you can stay next week while we're looking."

Matt was an instant away from blurting out his own plans for himself and Don, but Don spoke first. "I have to get a job," he said miserably. He was clinging to the idea as if it was the only thing keeping him from going under.

Meg suddenly lost control. "Don't keep saying that!" she yelled. "I *know* you do. Why do you think we've been—?"

"Shut up, Meg!" Matt told her furiously. "If you're going to make things worse, why don't you just get out of here?"

She stood up, her face turned away from them. "I'm going home," she said in a strangled voice. "Anyone want a ride?"

"No," Matt said coldly. "I'd rather walk."

Don looked unhappily from Matt to Meg, but he stayed where he was, his knees drawn up against his chest and his arms wrapped around them like a kid trying to make himself less noticeable while his parents are fighting.

Once he was alone with Don, Matt found he couldn't bring up the idea of their taking off together. Not yet. It would put a kind of jinx on tomorrow's job hunting and snuff out his last frail hope that they might not have to go. Time enough to discuss it tomorrow night. He stood up, yawning and stretching. "Coming?" he said to Don.

"I guess not. I'm going to sleep here tonight." Don had a sleeping bag in the tack room and often spent the night up there, especially when a sick horse or foaling mare needed watching. "Matt, we hurt Meg's feelings. It wasn't fair."

"I know," Matt admitted. "She and I both have tempers, Don, that's all. It'll be okay tomorrow. Don't worry about us."

Leaving Don in Cricket's stall, he started the long jog home. Except that it wasn't home. Home was the place where, when you went there, they had to let you in—like old Robert Frost said. He didn't have a place like that anymore. *You don't belong anywhere, McKendrick, and nobody owes you anything. Can't you get that through your thick skull?*

It was after eleven when he finally got in. The front lights were on, but Ryder's Mercedes was not in the garage. Thank God for that, anyway. Tiptoeing stealthily down the carpeted hallway to his bedroom, he did not close the door this time, but left his books on the desk and undressed in the dark to avoid advertising the fact that he was back.

One more day. That was all they had left. On Sunday, unless they got lucky, he and Don would be heading north.

172

23

It was still dark on Saturday morning when Matt took a street directory out of Sally's car and the want-ad section from the *Times* and rode the bus down Verde Canyon to the shopping center. In the coffee shop, fortified by two glasses of orange juice and a plate of eggs, he began going through the ads one by one, crossing each one off as he finished reading it. He wasn't expecting to find anything; he was doing it so he would know he had eliminated every other possibility before he took the last alternative open to them.

The black x's made by his pen crawled slowly down the columns. One page done. He wasn't looking for a job with animals anymore—just a job, either live-in like a night watchman, or high-paying enough to cover room and board separately. Three more finished. How many to go? He scanned the pages of black and white hieroglyphics, counting them, and the ad at the top of one of the last columns jumped out at him.

Vet nds lv-in asst. Apply 2095B Carob St. Sat 9-5.

With shaking hands, Matt looked up Carob on the street

map. He wouldn't care if it were in Culver City, but if it—
There it was! A four-block street not too far from Lowell.
A job! Animals, live-in—it was perfect!

He dropped the dime three times before he got it into
the pay phone. The phone rang for a long time at Don's
house before a growling male voice answered.

"Don?" Matt said uncertainly.

"The dummy ain't here. Who is this?"

Matt let the remark go. "When he comes in, tell him
Matt called. It's important."

"You got a nerve, getting me outta bed this hour in the
morning wanting me to take messages for that dummy. I
ain't no answering service!" The unknown man crashed
the receiver down.

Matt tried the stables next, but a cheerful Caesar said no,
Don wasn't there. No one was home at the Schuylers'
either. Only one thing to do.

Twenty minutes later he was standing on the front porch
of what had once been a single-family house. The street
had gradually been zoned commercial, and Dr. A. Vargas,
D.V.M., had renovated this house into a veterinary hospital and boarding kennel. He could use an assistant. The
house needed a coat of paint, and the plants in front looked
pretty scraggly.

At nine o'clock precisely, Matt rang the bell. The door
was opened by a small dark man wearing horn-rimmed
glasses, a goatee, and a long white coat. He looked inquir-
ingly at Matt.

"I, uh . . . I came about your ad."

"Ah, good. Come in, come in."

Matt followed the veterinarian through the waiting room and down past the examining rooms. The outside of the house might be shabby, but in here everything was spotlessly clean. Don would like working here . . . if he got the job. So much was riding on it, he had to. Oh lord, Matt thought, please let this work. . . .

Dr. Vargas began walking down a row of cages, letting every second dog into the outside runs for their morning exercise. "Mind giving me a hand?" he said, handing Matt a long-handled scoop. "I'm getting a late start this morning, as usual. It's one of the reasons I need someone to live in. Have you had any experience with animals?"

Matt had been preparing himself for this interview ever since he left the coffee shop at a run. The hardest part was going to be getting the vet to understand the situation before he got annoyed with Matt for wasting his time. "Yes, sir," he said rapidly, "but I'm not applying for this job myself. I came because of a friend."

Dr. Vargas had his back to Matt. For what seemed like forever, he said nothing. Oh lord, Matt thought miserably, have I blown it already?

The vet laughed. "He must be a good friend for someone your age to be up this early on a Saturday morning."

Matt let his breath out. "He is, and he's been looking for a job exactly like this one for weeks."

"How can you be so sure? This is not a glamorous job, you know. It means long hours, round-the-clock responsibility, and a lot of cleaning up after messy animals." He gestured at the loaded scoop in Matt's hand. "It's not a job for everyone."

"I know, but it's exactly what he's been doing—what he likes to do." Anxiety made the words run out like air from a punctured tire. "He's great with animals—any kind of animal. He's the kind of quiet, gentle guy animals trust, and he cares about them. He's been working at Las Lomas stables for the last three years for practically nothing, grooming and exercising. There's not a horse in the stable he can't make do what he wants, and lots of times he's spent the night with a mare in foal or a horse needing medication every three hours." Matt felt himself beginning to run down under the vet's faintly amused scrutiny. "He's the only one who can give some of the horses shots or calm them down so they can be shod, and—"

"Whoa!" Dr. Vargas was laughing as he started up the other row of cages. "How old is this wonder boy?"

Matt winced. Had he gone overboard describing Don? "He'll be eighteen tomorrow, and on his own."

"What about his family, and school?"

"No family. He wants to finish high school, but he graduates in January. Goes to Lowell."

A bell rang out in front. While Dr. Vargas was answering it, Matt continued working on the cages to keep his mind off what would happen when the vet came back. He was wondering whether there was anything else he should say or whether he had already said too much, when Vargas reappeared with a huge, fluffy, carrot-colored cat in his arms.

"Thanks for the help," he said. "I appreciate it. I can't decide anything until your friend comes to see me. Tell him I'll be here until five this afternoon, but I won't be in at all tomorrow."

176

"I'll tell him, sir. Thanks a lot! If you hire him—Don Turner's his name—I know you won't be sorry."

Matt was so high after the interview that he sprinted most of the way to Don's house. Pulse ticking rapidly in his throat, he rang the bell and waited impatiently for Don to come out and hear the great news.

The door was opened by a worn, middle-aged blonde in curlers and a food-spotted housecoat. "Don?" she repeated, glancing nervously over her shoulder and lowering her voice. "He didn't come in last night. I don't know where he is. Please, whoever you are, don't come around pestering us about him anymore. Arnie doesn't like it." She closed the door and left Matt on the doorstep, grinding his teeth in frustration.

Stopping at a gas station to phone the Schuylers and getting no answer, he tried the Ryders next. What if Don had been trying all this time to reach him? No one was home there, either. Where was everybody?

Forced to spend one of the six precious hours that were left riding the bus up to Las Lomas and leaving a note for Meg on the Schuylers' front door and tormented by the feeling that he was a couple of minutes behind Don at every stop, he caught another bus back to the shopping center and raced through all the stores. At the coffee shop he asked a waitress who knew them, but she hadn't seen Don either. He was going out of his mind.

At half past two he called Don's house again and got a string of curses from the unknown man before the phone was slammed down. The same to you, mister, in spades— Matt told him as he dialed Meg's number. It rang and rang, a hollow sound in an empty house. He was about to hang up when he heard the click and a faint "Hello?"

"Hello, hello? Is Meg there? I have to talk to her. Hurry!"

Twenty minutes later Meg had picked him up and they were cruising the streets around Lowell, staring down every alley, straining around every corner, watching for a big guy in a red windbreaker.

At four-thirty Matt thought of the library. The reference librarian said yes, Don had been there all day reading the want-ads. He had left half an hour ago, she said. In a hurry.

Sitting in the car in the library parking lot, Meg rested her forehead against the steering wheel for a moment. "Now what?" she said in a strained voice.

"I don't know. Wait—yes, I do. We'll go back to the vet's and tell him Don couldn't make it today, but he'll be there first thing on Monday. At least that way the vet won't think Don doesn't want the job." To have come so close and then lost it—it was too much.

They were turning the corner into Carob when they saw Don. He was striding rapidly along the sidewalk, looking at the numbers on the houses. Matt reached over to honk the horn, but Meg knocked his hand away.

"Wait," she said breathlessly, pulling over to the curb. "Look, Matt. Is that the place you went to this morning?"

Don was standing at the foot of 2095B, checking the number one more time against the paper in his hand. It was ten minutes before five.

"Yes, it is. Oh lord, Meg—"

They stared at each other for the space of several heart-beats before laughter—wild, incredulous laughter—erupted deep inside. Roaring through them like a whirlwind, it swept up and blew away all the pent-up emotions of the past week, leaving them weak and empty and at peace.

Letting his head fall back wearily against the headrest, Matt decided he might as well start rebuilding some of his burnt bridges. "Meg?" The only reply was a faint hiccup. "Listen, I'm sorry about the lousy way I've been acting all week."

"You weren't the only one who was a rat. I'm sorry too. We could both use lessons in Coping With Crisis."

"Yeah well, it wasn't only that. I'd made up my mind that if we couldn't get Don a job, I was going to take off with him. Head north for the lumber camps."

"Head north? Lumber camps—?" Her voice rose. "Matt, you weren't. You couldn't!"

He looked at her. In the small pale oval of her face, her eyes were huge and frightened. He hadn't expected that kind of reaction. "What else could I have done?" he said roughly. "Let them put him in some stinking mental institution while I went on living happily ever after at the Ryders'? No way!"

"Matt. . . ." Meg's hollow voice was like cold water on his hot skin. "What if he doesn't get this job?"

"He will," Matt said instantly, remembering this morning's conversation. Everything was in Don's favor, he was sure of it.

"What if somebody else already got the job? What if the doctor is another one like the Career Center woman?"

"He isn't," Matt said shortly. He wanted her to stop talking about it. The day seemed to grow colder.

A tense half-hour passed. "That's a good sign," Matt said, wanting reassurance as much as Meg. "If the vet didn't want him, he'd have said so by now, wouldn't he?" Getting no response, he glanced at her again. She was staring straight ahead, breathing hard, her fists clenched around the useless steering wheel. Tears glistened on her cheeks. What in the Sam Hill—?

She stiffened suddenly. "Matt—"

He turned swiftly, following her gaze. Don was walking down the sidewalk toward them.

24

As Don passed under a streetlight, they caught a glimpse of his face. His wide grin told them everything they wanted to know.

With a sound like a choked-off sob, Meg slowly relaxed her grip on the wheel. "Matt," she whispered, "don't let him know you saw the doctor first or anything."

"What?"

"He found it on his own. Let's leave it like that." She honked the horn and moved forward to meet him.

Matt leaned out his window. "Hey, good buddy, where have you been all day? We've been looking all—"

Don interrupted him exuberantly. "Hey, you guys, guess what? I got a job! It's perfect! You gotta see it! I can live there and finish school, and I get paid enough so I can eat. It's perfect!"

"Where? What kind of job?" Matt hoped he didn't sound as as phony as he felt.

"Hop in," Meg added. "Where are you heading now?"

"Back to the house to get my things. I can move in tonight. I can't believe it!" Talking nonstop, Don got into the back seat. "I read every ad in the paper. It took me almost all day, and this one was down at the end. It started with a 'V.' He's a vet, but he's got a boarding kennel, too. I get to do a lot of work with the animals, keep the place clean—"

For the first time in days, Matt was hearing one of his favorite sounds—Meg's mischievous, lighthearted giggle. "You really are something, Don," she said.

Don stopped talking as if she had clapped a hand over his mouth. When he began again he was very serious. "Do you mind? I mean, after all the work you did driving around all day and everything, and then—and I just—"

"Mind?" Matt hooted. "Are you crazy? I'm going home to sleep for twenty-four hours, and then we're going to celebrate!"

"You nut!" Meg said, laughing. "What do you mean, mind? What do you think we went through all that for in the first place? Hey, I know! Why don't we get your stuff and take it over right now since we're here?"

"You don't mind?"

"If you say that again, Don Turner," Meg told him fiercely, and she wasn't kidding, "you are going to get out and walk!"

He couldn't stop talking. Matt had never heard Don like this; his breathless words tumbled all over each other like kids shoving and pushing to get to the head of the line. It was the biggest and best thing that had ever happened to him, and he had done it entirely on his own.

Matt was only slightly less delirious himself. He was

free—home free, in more ways than one! He could go home tonight and share the whole terrible week with Ryder and Sally. He could go to sleep in his own bed in his own room knowing it wasn't the last night after all, and on Monday in seventh period he could start running like he'd never run before! For the last week he had been seeing his future through the wrong end of a telescope—himself and Don, two insignificant figures on a long lonely road to nowhere. Suddenly his life had opened up again, full of light and air and people he cared about and dreams he was not finished with after all. "Whoo-ee!" he exulted and was echoed immediately by the other two.

They drew up in the driveway of a shabby little stucco house. Don had never wanted them to see where he lived before, but now he didn't care. Still flying high on his tremendous victory, he hustled them through the front door. When he saw his foster mother in the living room, he gave her the news as if he expected her to be as excited as he was.

"Guess what, Aunt Cora? I got a job!"

She was sitting on the sofa, her feet up on a coffee table, a can of beer in her hand. Another can was making wet rings on the table beside her fuzzy pink slippers. "A job?" she repeated blankly. "Who's gonna hire a boy like you?"

Before Don could tell her, a short, heavyset man came out of the kitchen carrying a bag of pretzels. When he saw the three of them, his face grew ugly. "You the bastard who's been calling all day?" he said, advancing on Matt.

Matt did not appreciate the insult, but they were here to get Don's things and go. "I guess so," he said. "I'm sorry if—"

"Sorry!" the man snarled. "For two bits I'd take you apart here and now."

The telltale flush was spreading rapidly across Meg's cheekbones. "Matt," she said urgently.

"Arnie," the woman put in hastily, "Don says he's got a job."

"A job?" Arnie snorted. "You gotta be kidding. Did you tell them after next week you won't be around anymore?"

"It's the kind of job where I live there. You don't have to worry about me now, Aunt Cora."

If Matt hadn't been watching them, he would have missed the proud, fleeting smile that Don's foster mother sent him. It was followed instantly by a nervous glance at her boyfriend that spoke volumes. She loved Don, but he could not provide her with the things a man could, and Arnie was the only man she had.

Matt nudged Meg. "Get Don moving, will you?" he muttered.

"Well, big shot," the man said when they were alone, "you must think you're pretty terrific, huh? Getting the dummy a job all his own and—"

Matt could not take much more of this. "He got it himself," he said curtly.

"Watch yourself, kid!" Arnie was obviously spoiling for a fight. When Matt remained silent, he continued to bait him. "So what happens when he loses the job and turns up here again? What are we supposed to do with him then?"

Don's Aunt Cora plucked nervously at the man's sleeve. "Arnie, please—"

He brushed her off impatiently. "Stay outta this, Cora.

You never thought of that, did you, Mr. Big? We don't want him back here. No way. And he ain't gonna make it out there. He belongs in an institution with the other dummies like him."

Matt ground his teeth, fighting for control. How could anyone live with this constant put-down? No wonder Don was always so apologetic about causing him and Meg the slightest trouble.

"You better understand one thing," Arnie went on. "When that dummy walks outta here—"

"Don't call him that!" Matt said furiously. *You god-damn jerk! He's worth fifty of you!* Glancing up the hall, he saw Meg and Don coming at last. Just in time. One more minute and—

He saw it coming too late to duck. Arnie's fist smashed into his mouth, and his head hit the wall behind him with a crack. An instant later he was sinking like a stone through the darkness of a muddy pond. . . .

"Matt?" For a moment he did not recognize the frightened voice. "Matt, please—!"

"I'm okay," he said thickly.

"Can you get up?" Someone hauled on his arm, forcing him to sit and then to stand.

"Get him outta here!" A high volume voice battered at his aching head. "All of you get out, and don't any of you show your faces around here again!"

Matt leaned dizzily against a wall while the floor heaved under his feet. Distantly he heard Meg's voice, trembling with fury. "When we've got Don's things in the car, we'll go; and you don't have to worry about us coming back. Who would want to?"

His feelings exactly. And the sooner they got out of there the better. Stumbling outside with them, he propped himself against the car while the other two went back inside a couple of times for the few things Don had managed to collect and save in his eighteen years. Enough to fill six Safeway bags. Before they drove away, Meg made Matt stretch out on the back seat. His head was killing him, but he could live with that kind of pain. Compared to the agony of the last week, it was peanuts.

When he roused himself again, he found the car parked on Carob. Except for himself, it was empty. A few minutes went by before Meg got into the front seat and leaned over it to inspect him.

"Matt, are you really okay? You don't look too—"

"I'm okay." The words, banging around inside his skull, made him wince. "Just get me home," he whispered.

She got him home in record time, parking the car and coming around to open the door as if he were a doddering invalid. "See you Monday," she said casually, but he could feel her eyes on his back until he opened the front door.

He stumbled over the threshhold, concentrating on holding his head perfectly still so it wouldn't fall and shatter into a thousand pieces. He was not worried about being quiet, but he thought he'd put off his conversation with Sally and Ryder until tomorrow. He wasn't feeling too coherent right now.

As the door banged shut behind him, a hand came down on his shoulder. "Matt, come into the library . . . please."

The *please* did not soften the impact of Ryder's flint-edged voice on Matt. He preceded the lieutenant into the

186

dim room, which was lit only by the faint glow of a dying fire in the big stone fireplace. Oh lord, he was thinking, I must have done a better job of burning my bridges than I thought.

Behind him, Ryder closed the door. "Well?"

Matt turned to face him, grateful for the semi-darkness. "Sir?"

"Do you have any explanation?"

Rubbing the bone above his eyes to ease the throbbing in his head, Matt tried to think. What should he explain first? Was there anything that couldn't wait? "Sir, I'm sorry. What do you want me to explain?"

Eyes narrowed, Ryder gazed at him for a long time. Chills began to shake Matt's body. "You really did forget, didn't you? I never would have thought it possible."

"What? I don't—"

"Today," Ryder said, and there was nothing gentle about that cold, deliberate voice, "was Michael's birthday."

"Michael's birth—?" *Oh Michael . . . oh God, no!*

A vision of his own glorious birthday celebration filled Matt's pounding head. It had been one of the great days of his life, full of laughter and teasing and surprises. And love. They had done all that for him—a stranger, a guest in their house—and today had been Michael's turn to be celebrated and surprised and told how glad they all were he had been born. He had not just forgotten Michael's birthday, he had destroyed it.

Thinking there might still be time to give Michael his present, he started for the door, but Ryder stopped him. "It's too late, Matt. Sally finally got him quieted down an

187

hour ago." Ryder paused, waiting for Matt to turn and look at him. "We came home from the beach at three-thirty this afternoon. He's been crying since four o'clock."

Matt saw it all, saw every moment as if he had been there. Michael asking anxiously all the way home whether Matt would be there waiting for him, racing through the house calling his name in a voice growing shriller and more desperate as the truth became clear, and then, bewildered and hurt, surrounded by the streamers and balloons and brightly wrapped presents, sobbing inconsolably. It was his great day and his best brother had not come home to celebrate it with him. *Oh Michael, how could I have done such a lousy thing to you?*

"I'm still waiting for some kind of explanation."

Ryder's remote voice shook Matt badly. They were on opposite sides again. He was the outsider who had hurt Ryder's son, and Ryder was going to find out why. Nausea contracted his stomach muscles and rose into the back of his throat. Concentrating hard, he fought it down.

"I can give you the only explanation I thought of," Ryder went on relentlessly, "but you won't like it. I don't like it myself." He paused. "You've been sulking ever since I vetoed your plan to have us adopt—"

"Not adopt," Matt protested feebly. It seemed like an important point, if he could just collect his thoughts—

"—adopt your friend, and you've been acting like a spoiled brat all week. Leaving home early, getting in late. Cutting classes. Avoiding all of us. It isn't like you, Matt, but it's the only answer I've been able to come up with. And it sure as hell doesn't justify what you did today. Am I wrong?"

188

Matt wished desperately for a way to open his mouth and have everything—the whole truth—come out in one neat package for Ryder to understand all at once. It was so complicated, and his head—

"For Christ's sake, Matt!" Ryder roared, scaring Matt so badly that his mind went absolutely blank. "I'm asking you a question and I expect an answer!"

"I—we didn't—we only had a week to find Don a job and—"

"Is that what you've been doing all week?"

Matt nodded and instantly wished he hadn't. "We went everywhere looking—Don and Meg and me." He was going to be sick any second. He had to wrap this up in a hurry. "He found one today. We were helping him move his things."

"And that was more important to you than Michael's birthday?"

"No, sir. I—" A wave of heat was coming up from the floor, turning him inside out as it came. "I can't—" He wrenched the door open and raced down the long hall, barging past Sally as she came out of the kitchen. Slamming the bathroom door behind him, he was violently ill into the toilet.

Someone knocked on the door and called his name while he was trying to catch his breath. By the time he had cleaned up as well as he could and opened the door, they were gone. He made it into his room with some help from the walls and fell onto the bed. Undressing was out of the question.

"Matt?" Someone wanted him again. He wished they would leave him alone. "Matt, what's wrong?"

Why did people keep asking him that? "Okay," he mumbled. "I'm okay."

No one was there when he dragged his eyes open, but the overhead light was on. He tried to roll on his side away from its piercing brightness. A hand on his shoulder held him still. Squinting up, he saw Ryder and Sally.

Ryder's face moved closer. "Have you been in a fight?"

"No," he said indistinctly, and flinched as Ryder's voice came crashing down around his head.

"For God's sake, Matt, don't lie to me on top of everything else! You have a lip on you like a prize-fighter. Where did you get it?"

"Les!" Sally said sharply.

"Not a fight. Guy . . . hit me. Once. Banged head on . . . on. . . ." He could not remember. "I'm okay," he said, making a tremendous effort to sound as if he was. "Happened before. Head like a rock. Be okay tomorrow."

He was vaguely aware that he was being taken care of. Ryder helped him undress and tucked him between the cool sheets as if he were a little kid. Sally brought him a damp washcloth to sooth his burning head. But gradually, as if Sally and Ryder were on the shore and he was floating in the sea, he felt himself drifting away. Slowly at first, then faster and faster. Struggling against the inexorable current, he yelled for help, but the beach was empty. No one was listening anymore. No one was there.

25

Matt's first conscious thought on Sunday morning was that he had to find Michael fast. If he could explain how yesterday happened and make Michael understand that it was a terrible mistake and not something he had done on purpose, it might ease Michael's pain a little, even if it wouldn't change what he had done.

No one was home except Mrs. B. She was in her room, dressed to go out and waiting to see how he felt before she left him alone. The lieutenant and Sally had taken the children to Disneyland, she informed him brusquely, to make up a little for yesterday's disappointment. After satisfying herself that he was well enough to look after himself, she left for her weekly visit to her sister's. The Ryders would not be back until late, but there was cold roast beef for his supper.

Her sharpness towards him was an echo of Ryder's, leaving no doubt about the way they felt. Gary had been right. He *was* the kind of guy who could hurt someone **he** loved. If he had deliberately set out to make them change their minds about him, he could not have found a better way.

He had a lot of time to kill until Michael got home. Clearing a place to do some homework, he shoved aside the stack of books he had dropped on his desk in the dark last Friday night and got the worst jolt yet.

On a large piece of drawing paper, Michael had painstakingly drawn a series of pictures of himself and Matt. From top to bottom the paper was covered with cartoon-like boxes showing Boo and rides on Buster and beach picnics and the early morning runs with Michael bicycling beside him. Written in between the boxes like a string connecting all their best times together was an invitation to Michael's birthday.

To my best brother, it said. *Please come to my party tomorrow. From your best brother Michael.* A P.S. was crammed into the bottom corner. *Don't forget.*

Matt suddenly wanted to get to Disneyland somehow and find them. Michael must be bleeding to death inside. His apology was the only thing that would close the wound and start it healing, and the longer it took him to say he was sorry, the longer it would take to heal.

But the odds of finding four people in the mob scene at that sprawling park were ridiculously small. By the time he got there it would be late afternoon, and if they came home before he did, it would only make things worse.

He had remained in the same position for so long that Cat, looking for company and getting no response, climbed up his pant leg and then his shirt to his shoulder, draping herself like a fur piece across the back of his neck. The soft warmth of her body and the steady rumble of her purring

192

comforted him a little. "You're lucky, Cat," he told her as his gaze fell on two small packages sitting on the bookshelf in front of him. "You don't make anyone anything but happy."

One of the packages was Michael's present, wrapped and waiting, proof that he hadn't forgotten the great day completely. The other had a brown paper wrapping and had been mailed from Idaho over a week ago. It could have been there for days for all he knew.

Inside the wrapping was a small square box crammed full of tissue paper and so light Matt thought at first it was empty. His searching fingers finally found a piece of notebook paper folded tightly around something hard and lumpy. As he unfolded the paper, the object clattered to his desk.

It was a small gold medal, no bigger than a quarter, on a long chain. The first medal he had ever won in a running event. His mom had put it on a chain for him, but he had been too embarrassed to wear it. It seemed too much like showing off, and she had never done it again.

Where had it come from? Matt spread the notebook paper out flat. The handwriting was unmistakable. *I looked everywhere,* Gary had written. *Found this one snagged on a dead tree. Guess the rest are gone. Sorry, Matt.*

Sorry, Matt—? With a swift gesture Matt crumpled the note and flung it and the medal into a wastebasket, but a sudden impulse made him retrieve the medal and toss it into the back of a drawer instead. *Forget you, Maitland! After what you did, a "sorry" and that lousy little piece of metal are supposed to make everything okay? No way.*

193

Trying to distract himself from anxiety about Michael and his own future as a member of the Ryders' household, he spent the rest of the long afternoon catching up on work he had neglected during the past week, but the effort of concentrating proved hard on his head. He went to bed early and was so deep in sleep when the Ryders came home that not even Jenny's shouts woke him. When Meg came by for him the next morning, he went out and told her he would take the bus. He could not let another day go by without telling Michael how sorry he was. He was bleeding to death himself.

He had put the little present in the middle of Michael's breakfast plate. Mrs. B looked at it without comment, and Sally, when she came in, simply asked if he felt well enough to go to school. He was so finely tuned to their reactions that he thought he heard an unaccustomed edge to Sally's voice. He had finally dropped a stone into the well of her understanding that was too big to be absorbed. Oh lord, he was thinking miserably when Michael came into the kitchen and slid silently into his seat.

Suddenly Matt knew he had made a mistake. In here, with Sally and Mrs. B listening, was not the right place for telling Michael how he felt about what he had done. He should have invited Michael into his room. They should have been lying on his bed, Michael's feet on the wall and his head on Matt's stomach, talking it over and getting it all straightened out.

"What's this?" Michael asked his mother.

Matt cleared his throat. "It's your birthday present. I'm really sorry about Saturday, Michael. I can't believe I did such a lousy thing to you, but it was a mistake. I didn't do it on purpose, if you can—" He stopped.

Michael had lifted the small box off his plate and shoved it across the table at Matt. "I don't want it," he said flatly. "It's not my birthday anymore."

Matt rose unsteadily. Why didn't Sally and Mrs. B get out of the kitchen and leave them alone? He stared at the little present in its bright wrapping and at Michael's blond head, now bent in elaborate concentration over his plate of scrambled eggs.

"I don't blame you for being mad," he said quietly. "I guess it's not much good to you now, my saying I'm sorry, but I am." Michael gazed at Matt over the rim of his orange juice glass, a remote distant look like his father's. You're right, Matt was thinking. Apologies don't help. They don't make any difference at all. "I'll keep it for you then. If you change your mind, it'll be on my desk."

When he came home that afternoon, he saw immediately that Michael had not changed his mind. The present was still there on the shelf, but the birthday invitation had vanished from the wall where Matt had taped it. Upset by its loss, he went to Michael's room and challenged him with its disappearance. "What did you do with it?"

"I tore it up in a million pieces," Michael said sullenly.

"You shouldn't have done that. It was mine. I wanted to keep it."

"It was mine. I made it, and I didn't want it anymore."

"Don't ever come into my room like that when I'm not there and take anything again."

"I can do what I want with my own stuff," Michael

said shrilly, "and anyway I made a mistake. You aren't my real brother. You just live here." Matt's face told Michael he had scored a direct hit. As Matt abruptly left the room, he followed it up with another, stronger one. "I wish you'd go somewhere else to live!"

Matt closed his bedroom door and locked himself in with the sleeping Cat. He did not want anyone coming in unexpectedly and seeing him white and shaken. It was too late for explanations. Explanations would not make Michael feel differently about him. Too late to say he was sorry; what he had done could not be undone. He had not only hurt his little brother, he had made Michael hate him. He could not go on living here under those conditions. He wouldn't want to, knowing their feelings for him had changed. You'll get your wish, Michael, he was thinking. It won't be long now.

26

It might have happened right away if Christmas had not intervened. He had been too preoccupied with the search for Don's job to notice it coming. Now it was only a couple of weeks away, and everyone was too busy to worry about him. He tried to settle down and make the most of his last few days, but the season itself proved his undoing.

Because it was the one time of year when the same things were traditionally done in the same ways, Christmas memories were the clearest of all. The carols reminded him of sleigh rides and Christmas Eve at the Maitlands' and Katie's triumphant mastery of "Jingle Bells." The smells from Mrs. B's baking brought back visions of his whole family in the kitchen decorating sugar cookies and gingerbread men to take to friends; and the search for exactly the right tree in the vast acreage of an evergreen farm nearly drove him out of his mind.

The voices of other families calling to each other through the trees took on a familiar ring. He kept mistaking them for voices he knew, kept hearing echoes of his own family and friends. Taking refuge in the car, he huddled in the front seat with the windows closed and the radio on as loudly as he could stand it, but he was helpless against the flood of memories pouring over him and in the end he broke down and cried.

Michael acted as if he were not there at all; and although Jenny remained on friendly terms with him, she kept asking him questions he couldn't answer. Where did he come from? Why was he living with them if he had another mommy and daddy? Was he ever going to go away and live somewhere else? Matt wasn't sure whether she had heard Michael or her parents talking about him, but he hated the questions. In an effort to keep out of everyone's way, he spent less and less time at the Ryders'.

Eating a hurried breakfast, he would leave immediately for the Schuylers' and school, returning home late enough each day so the two small Ryders would be through with supper and he could eat by himself. A couple of afternoons he spent with Don, drilling him on the labels in Vargas' medicine cabinet, in case he was ever asked to give an animal medication at night; and the rest of the time he was up at the Schuylers'. It was the only place where he did not have to pretend that everything was going great.

He had told Will and Meg about the birthday disaster and Michael's reaction. As the strain of waiting for the ax to fall became harder for him to handle, he admitted his fears about the future as well. Everything came to a head on one of the rare aftenoons when he and Meg were the only ones home.

He was stretched full-length on the family room floor, staring sightlessly at the ceiling, while Meg moved around him straightening up. What the hell am I hanging around for? he asked himself suddenly. I know what's going to happen. Why wait? "I'm leaving," he said, immensely relieved now that the decision had been made.

Whatever kind of reaction he was expecting, it wasn't the one he got. Meg froze, one hand still reaching for an empty glass. "Leaving?" she repeated. "You mean running away—again?"

He did not like the way that sounded. "Yes," he said shortly.

Suddenly she seemed years older, cold and distant. "Are you going to tell them?"

"Tell who?"

"The Ryders. That you're leaving."

"That's a dumb question."

"Are you?"

"No!"

"Just going to walk out on everybody without saying good-bye, is that it? You're pretty good at that, aren't you?"

He never should have started this conversation. "Forget I said anything," he said sharply. "I figured you'd be—"

"Sympathetic? I am, but it's not you I feel sorry for."

"That's not what I—"

"You can't do it, Matt. Not this time."

"Don't start the Big Mother bit with me, Meg. You can't run my life the way you do everyone else's around here."

"Yes I can, Matt. This time I can, and I'm going to."

"Like hell—"

"Either you're going to tell them," she said flatly, "or I am."

He was on his feet at once. "Like hell you are!"

"Like hell I am! I'll do it, Matt, if I have to. It's up to you."

Up to him? She had him backed into a corner and she was telling him he had a choice? "I've taken a lot of bullying from you, Meg Schuyler, but nobody blackmails me into doing something I don't want to do. You're not telling the Ryders a damn thing!"

"I won't have to if you do it yourself." She met his gaze coolly, but the color in her cheeks gave her real feelings away.

"You know something?" he said bitterly. If she had been a foot taller and male, he would have flattened her. "You're too damn tough for your own good!"

"I have to be," she snapped, her green eyes sparking dangerously. "Nobody else around here is."

Abruptly he swung around and headed for the door. The sooner he got out of here, the better.

"If you go out that door, Matt McKendrick, without promising you'll talk to the Ryders tonight, then as soon as you shut it I'm calling Sally."

He could not believe this. What *right* did she have? "Meg, if you—!"

"And if you don't tell them tonight, I'll tell them myself tomorrow!"

He stared at her, speechless and infuriated.

"Promise?"

What choice did he have? Jesus, he hated her!

"Promise, Matt! I mean it."

"I'll do it!" he said savagely. "I'll do it because I have to, you witch, and not because I want to!" He was halfway down the front walk when he whirled around. She was standing in the doorway, watching him go. "Damn you, Meg Schuyler! Damn you to hell!"

Wound up like a time bomb, armed and ready to explode, Matt was waiting in the garage when Ryder got home at seven. "Sir," he said tensely, ignoring the lieutenant's greeting, "I have to talk to you before dinner. It's important." As Ryder hesitated, he added, "It won't take long."

Ryder led the way down to the library, Matt following closely on his heels. This time it was Matt who closed the door.

"Sir," he said without preamble, "I want to leave—go somewhere else to live."

The lighted match in Ryder's hand was halfway to the cigarette in his mouth. He studied Matt for a moment, then shook out the match and dropped the unlighted cigarette into an ashtray, giving Matt his full attention. "Are you asking me or telling me?"

"Telling you, I guess."

"Are you going to tell me why?"

"You know why."

"I do?"

"I don't belong here anymore, that's why."

Ryder was dumbfounded. "I don't believe I'm hearing this! What makes you think you don't belong?"

Jesus—! The old interrogation room bit. Ryder was going to make him sweat this one out. Well, all right. If he wanted the whole truth, he could have it.

"I'm just a stray, a kid in trouble that you took in when there was no place else for me to go. A lousy gutless wonder who can't stand on his own feet—"

"Matt—"

"—and you and Sally have done at lot for me in spite of it. Don't think I'm not grateful, but I know you don't owe me anything. I'm not your son and—"

"Matt—!"

"I've been nothing but trouble for you ever since I came—ever since you've known me—and now, after what I did to Michael and everything, I—"

"*Matt!*" Ryder roared. "Stop talking and listen to me!"

Matt stopped abruptly, his mouth still open.

"Are you out of your mind? A stray? A gutless wonder? Matt, for Christ's sake, where did you get all that bull?"

"It's the truth!"

"It's bullshit! You think you're some homeless animal we picked up off the street, something we're going to take up in the hills and turn loose if we change our minds? You don't have much faith in human nature, or yourself, do you?"

"Sir, I—"

"You call yourself a gutless wonder? You? A kid with a stubborn sense of justice that won't let you back down no matter how bad the odds? That sends you into battle for friends and strangers and occasionally—but not often enough, damn it—for yourself, regardless of the consequences? A kid with the toughness and courage to survive the worst that can happen to a human being and still be capable of laughing at yourself and feeling compassion for other people?"

"Sir—"

"And as for trouble—you're so damned determined to

keep your troubles to yourself that I'm lucky to even find out about them, let alone be of any help." Taking a couple of deep breaths, Ryder got himself under control. His voice calmer, he went on. "You're right about one thing, Matt. Just one. You aren't my son. But I wish to hell you were." He reached for Matt suddenly, getting a firm grip on each shoulder as if afraid of losing him before he finished what he had to say.

"Matt, listen to me. This is important, the most important thing I've ever said to you. After all the time we've put in planning how to ask you, Sally would never forgive me if I botched it up now. Are you listening?"

Matt nodded speechlessly. If it were anyone else who was telling him this, he would not have believed what he was hearing either. But Ryder— In all the time he had known him, Lieutenant Ryder had never lied to him . . . and had never said anything he didn't mean.

"I'm no good at telling people how I feel about them, I know that. Someday I'll tell you why. But I'm not like Sally and Tony. It's probably my fault you've been carrying this junk around in your head for so long." He paused. "Matt—not a day goes by that I don't thank God you are who you are, that you stood up to me when I was wrong and gave me a chance to make up a little for the hell I put you through. I don't owe you anything? That's bullshit too. It's you who owe me nothing." He gave Matt a gentle shake. "You won't hear me say this very often, Matt. It doesn't come easily, but I'm thinking it all the time. I want you to know that, remember it. All right?"

Matt nodded again.

"I love you. Can you get that through that stubborn, independent head of yours and keep it there? I love you, and so does everyone else in this house. Almost since the day you arrived we've wanted to adopt you, take the last legal step to make you one of the family. But it's like a marriage proposal. We've been afraid of choosing the wrong time to ask. Matt, is it too soon?"

If Ryder's big hands had not held him so firmly where he was, Matt would have turned away to hide the sudden rush of feeling. Staring into Ryder's strong angular face, he felt himself coming undone inside. All the uncertainty about himself—the need to know and have it settled that had consumed him for so long—was coming up and out with the tears sliding down his cheeks.

Ryder's grip increased slightly. "Well, Matt?" he said gently. "Is it?"

A weak grin fought its way past the gigantic lump in Matt's throat. They wanted him. They wanted *him!* Wordlessly he shook his head. An instant later Ryder was squeezing the air out of his lungs with a bear hug as exuberant and painful as one of Tony Prado's.

Releasing him suddenly, Ryder was at the door in a single stride. "Stay here, Matt. I want to get Sally. She's been waiting for this for a long time!"

Adopt him? Make it legal? Hey, Mr. Frost, he thought incredulously as he heard Sally's running footsteps coming down the hall. Guess what? Home isn't where they have to let you in. It's where they want to, even when they know who you are.

Oh man—! Oh *man*, am I a lucky guy!

27

Matt stopped by Don's the next afternoon to tell him the great news and got home while Michael and Jenny were having their supper. Last night, after Sally made sure he knew how she felt about his glorious decision, he and Sally and Ryder had stayed in the library for hours talking things over and clearing up all the misunderstandings. Mrs. B had finally brought supper in to them.

They had talked for a long time about Michael. "But we've all hurt people we love, Matt," Sally said finally. "It's what we do about it afterwards that makes the difference." She had promised to sound Michael out today at lunch to see whether it was anger at Matt or something else that was upsetting him so much, and Matt had been hoping to talk to her before he spoke to Michael himself, but he was out of luck. She had an assignment in the afternoon, and as he came up the drive, he saw that her car was still out.

Passing the kitchen door with a cheerful "Hi, everybody," he went straight to his room, thinking she might have left him a note. The first thing he saw was the picture.

Except for the message, it was a careful duplication of the *Best Brother* one. This one said in very small letters in the bottom right-hand corner, *I am srooy. Love Michael.* Laughing, mostly from sheer relief, Matt went into the kitchen. Mrs. B gave him a quick hug and asked if he could wait until the Ryders ate or wanted supper now.

"I can wait, Mrs. B, thanks." Going around behind Michael's chair, he whispered in his ear, "Thanks, best brother. I'm sorry too."

"What's the secret?" Jenny demanded. "I want to know too."

Thinking fast, Matt whispered, "You're terrific, but don't tell anybody."

Returning to his room, he turned out the light and after resettling Cat on the pillow, stretched out on his bed in the semi-darkness. He had learned from experience that when you want to talk about important things, it's easier to do it in the dark. He waited, thinking of times when he and Katie and—anyway, times when they had all waited motionless for hours to watch does bring their new fawns to drink at Little Creek.

There was a slight movement in the doorway. Matt did not respond right away. He had the same sensation as at Little Creek—a too-sudden approach or a too-direct question would be a disaster. "Hi," he said softly to the ceiling. "I was hoping you'd come."

As if someone had cut ropes restraining him, Michael shot across the room and flung himself on the bed. Burying his face in Matt's shirt, he cried tears he had held back for so long they seemed to have reached the boiling point as they soaked through the cloth to Matt's skin. Hugging his sobbing little brother, Matt waited patiently, glad it was all coming out. He knew how Michael felt.

At last Michael grew calmer. Rolling over, he put his head on Matt's stomach and his feet on the wall, as if to emphasize that all those awful days were over and they were taking up where they had left off.

"I missed you," Matt said after a while.

"I missed you more."

Matt thought that over. "I thought you wanted me to leave."

Michael's voice was very small. "Just for a little while I did. But when you didn't come home after school anymore, I was scared. I thought I'd made you hate me."

Matt's sudden laughter made Michael's head bounce. "Oh lord, Michael . . . you mean all that time I was thinking you hated me, you were thinking I hated you? And all the time we were hiding from each other, it was because we didn't know how to tell each other we were sorry? What a pair of nuts!"

Michael giggled. Remembering something else, he stretched his arm out over Matt's head. "Thanks for my birthday present." The watch strap was too large for his bony little wrist, and Matt got out his pocket knife and punched a couple of extra holes in it.

He felt as if he'd been on a long, dangerous ride through white water. Now he was past it, floating calmly into safe harbor. Sally was right. Telling someone you were sorry did make a difference. To him and Michael, it made all the difference in the world.

28

Matt had not seen Meg for three days. Either she was avoiding him or she was cutting classes, but she did not call to ask if he wanted a ride on Monday morning. He was happy to keep things that way.

It was true that if it hadn't been for her, he would not have brought things to a head and discovered how wrong he had been about the Ryders' feelings for him; but she couldn't have known how they were going to react. She had turned on him for some unknown reason, and it would be a long time before he felt like trusting her again.

Tuesday morning Will cornered him on the bus to school. He had a bruised look around the eyes as if he hadn't been getting enough sleep. "What the Sam Hill is going on between you and Meg?" he demanded as soon as they found a seat.

"It's none of your business—"

Will cut him off angrily. "It *is* my business. I have to live with her. If you think you've seen her in bad moods, you haven't seen anything yet. At dinner last night, Lew threw his fork at the wall and screamed that if he had to choose between her and you, he'd take you every time. Carey's in tears every ten minutes, and I'm about ready to move out. Without you around to prop up the weak timbers, the entire Schuyler family is falling apart."

Without him around—? First Ryder, then Michael, and now Will—each of them seeing him so differently from the way he thought they did, so differently from the way he'd been seeing himself. There may have been times when he was down to a leaky bathtub and half a paddle, but it looked as if the old Matt McKendrick hadn't been blasted out of the water for good after all.

Matt grinned. "Sorry about that, friend," he said lightly. "I thought all the propping up was being done by you guys."

"Well it wasn't, and you can't quit now. You may not need propping these days, but we sure do."

"I need it, I need it!" If he was ever going to tell Will how he felt about what they'd done for him, now was the time. "I owe you guys a lot."

"Sure you do. All kinds of good stuff like hassles and housework. And harangues . . . and harassments, and—"

"Horses and hospitality," Matt said before things got out of hand. For a moment they were silent, thinking about the last few months.

"Listen, Will," Matt said finally. "This thing with Meg— I can't explain it. Ask her to, if she can."

"I did. She just says she's scared she did something terrible to you, but she had to take the chance and Mom would

209

have understood. Which means she was probably messing around in your life like a typical busybody, right?"

Matt nodded. "Look, I'm not going to give you the details. I don't even want to think about it anymore. If you want to tell her it worked out all right in the end, you can. I don't trust myself near her right now."

"Forget Meg," Will said abruptly. She must be in top form to make him so unsympathetic. "How about taking in a movie on Friday with Lew and Carey and me?"

"Friday? Isn't that Christmas Eve?"

"Oh . . . yeah. How about Thursday, then?"

"Okay." As long as Meg wasn't coming. "If I can get Sally's car, I'll drive."

"Great! To borrow a phrase—thanks, friend. Once Lew and Carey know you're still around, they won't find Meg so hard to take."

Wednesday afternoon was the beginning of Christmas vacation. Matt and Dr. Vargas had with great difficulty persuaded Don to take some time off before the holiday rush began. He loved the clinic and was so concerned about every animal in it that he hated to leave them for more than an hour at a time. He and Matt had decided to go out to Venice and fool around on the beach, but Meg was waiting for Matt outside the locker room door.

She looked terrible. Her face was pale, the skin around her eyes puffy and swollen, and her hair was dry and brittle as old straw. Had she been sick last week? Was that the reason she had blown up at him? If it was—

"Matt," she said, "I need to talk to you." It came out sounding more like a command than a request, and his reaction to that tone was immediate and instinctive.

"I can't right now. Be right there, Don," he yelled, so she would know he had something urgent waiting.

Looking around, Meg saw Don at his usual place by the gate. The message could not have been clearer. When she looked at him again, her eyes had filled with tears. Like him, though, she was too full of pride and prickly self-reliance to beg for something, no matter how much she wanted it.

"Forget it," she said bitterly. "Just forget it. I don't know why I thought you could help anyway."

"Neither do I," he said lightly. He had no intention of fighting with her in a place as public as this.

"Damn you," she said softly. "I hate you, too." A moment later she was heading for the parking lot at a run.

"Couldn't she come?" Don asked when Matt came jogging up.

"I didn't ask her," he said shortly. "Let's get going."

He got home after seven that night, tired and sandy and, as usual after spending any time with Don, feeling relaxed and unwound. The anger and the tension that had built up over the last weeks was almost gone, and he felt bad about what had happened that afternoon at school. After supper he might take a run up to the Schuylers' and see if Meg was there.

Mrs. B met him in the front hall. "Matthew, is Meg with you?" Matt shook his head. "Oh dear. Will has been calling since half past five. Are you sure she isn't with you?" she asked again, as if Meg could have been tucked absent-mindedly into his pocket like someone else's ball point pen. "The lieutenant and Sally have gone up there. Mr. Schuyler, poor man, is beside himself with worry."

Let him worry, Matt was thinking as he made a quick stop in his bedroom before heading up to the Schuylers' at a run. It might do him good for a change. And Meg too.

Ryder had already called downtown and alerted Juvenile Division and Missing Persons. L.A. was a chancy place for young girls out alone at night. Will showed Matt the note Meg had left. *Take care of yourselves for a while*, it said. *I'll be back when I'm ready.*

"She's had enough," Matt told them. Everyone was listening, but it was Meg's father he was talking to. Meg needed him. Maybe it wouldn't make any difference to Mr. Schuyler if he knew that, but it might. It was worth a try. "She's had all she can take of being head cook and housekeeper and chauffeur and substitute mother around here. With all of us down on her, this week has been the last straw." That part of it was his fault more than any-one else's. It was up to him to do something about it. "I think I know where she's gone."

"I called the stable," Will said. "They haven't seen her."

"They wouldn't—not if she didn't want them to."

"I'll take you up there, Matt," Mr. Schuyler said un-expectedly. "If you have anything else to say, I'd like to hear it."

Matt had a lot to say. He said it all on the way there, while Mr. Schuyler listened, nodding thoughtfully and ask-ing questions that showed he was taking it all in. Meg wasn't going to like it when she knew what Matt had done, but he would face that problem when he came to it. For now he was not sorry he had taken a chance on her father.

Once at the stable, he made sure Meg was there before

212

asking Mr. Schuyler not to wait. Knowing her father needed to talk to Meg as much as he did, Matt was afraid he would want to begin at once, but Mr. Schuyler thanked him quietly and said he had a lot of things to think through. He would be grateful if Matt would bring Meg home in an hour or so. "Tell her—" he began, and stopped, adding as if to himself, "No, I'll tell her myself . . . if it's not too late. Thank you, Matt, and good luck."

Entering Cricket's stall by way of the paddock and the outside door, Matt found the gelding's silver-gray bulk taking up half the stall as he lay on his side asleep. Meg's pale face was visible in the corner, the rest of her a dark shadow easily overlooked by someone glancing through the feed bin window. Careful not to wake the sleeping horse, Matt worked his way around to where she was sitting and lowered himself to the shavings beside her. She turned her back on him. Not a good sign, he thought. Don't blow this, McKendrick, whatever you do.

"Meg?" he began uncertainly. Cricket stirred, and he lowered his voice. "We've all been unfair, haven't we? I thought it was just your father, expecting you to take your mom's place, but it's all of us, isn't it? Especially me."

Silence. *Keep trying, McKendrick.*

"It's your own fault, you know." He hoped she could tell by the sound of his voice that he was grinning. "You're so darned efficient. A born busybody—like your mother, Will says. Did I ever tell you—the first day we met, I thought you were about twenty years old?"

He was playing a riddle game where you got the prize if you came up with the right question, only he didn't know

213

which questions to ask. He didn't know which one, out of all the things that had gone wrong, was the straw that had broken her resistance. He wished she would give him a clue.

"Matt?"

Was it wishful thinking, or had he heard that muffled whisper? "Yeah?"

"What happened?"

"What?"

"The Ryders. What did they say?"

If that was the biggest question on her mind right now, then the hunch he'd had this afternoon was probably right. She'd had a pretty good idea of what they'd say—what Sally would say anyway. She and Sally had done a lot of talking last summer at the pool. She had forced him to find out how they felt because she knew they loved him. And he had called her a witch and damned her to hell. Oh lord. . . .

"They said exactly what you knew they'd say," he told her. "You are a witch—a nice one. You can read people's minds." He had been hoping to get a laugh out of her. It was a moment or two before he realized she was crying. Hard. "Hey," he said hastily, "it's okay. Everything's okay now. Michael, too." He wished he could put his arms around her to comfort her, but he wasn't sure how she'd react. "We got everything all straightened out. They want to adopt me."

Meg sat up, still sniffling. "Are you going to change your name?" she whispered.

"No."

"I didn't think you'd want to. I wasn't sure whether you'd have to or not."

"I can choose because I'm over the age of consent or something. Maybe if things had been different—I mean I wouldn't mind being a Ryder, only. . . ." His voice trailed off.

Meg finished the thought. "Only it would be too much like hiding."

"Yes, that. And being the last one in my family. Mc-Kendrick is too good a name to throw away. They understand."

They were silent for a while. Then Meg stirred and sighed. "Matt, I'm sorry I was so horrible on Thursday—no, wait," she said as he started to interrupt. "I want to tell you. I knew how Sally felt, but I wasn't sure about Lieutenant Ryder. I was taking a big chance, making you tell him. What if he'd said 'Okay, go if you want to'? It would have been your whole life I'd ruined. I was scared to death the whole time—scared of losing you if I didn't make you do it, and scared of losing you if I did. And when I'm scared I get mad. Mad and mean. I'm sorry."

"Don't be. If you hadn't done it, I might have been on my way to nowhere right now. And speaking of running away, Miz M. Schuyler—"

"I said I was coming back."

"Yeah, but in the meantime you've got everyone in a panic."

"They can manage all right without me," she said shortly.

"No, they can't. Neither can I. If you don't know that

by now, you're as blind as I am." What was wrong with him? All he wanted to do was put his arm around her, for crying out loud, and he was in a sweat because she might resent it. Tell him to cut it out or something. He'd never felt this way with her before—shy and awkward and nervous.

Come on, McKendrick, take a chance. Tentatively, ready to retrieve it instantly if she resisted, he draped his right arm across her shoulders. Either she had small shoulders or he had a long arm, because there seemed to be a lot of him left over. Half his arm was dangling out there in the darkness in front of her face, growing longer by the second. And heavier. What was he supposed to do now? If she didn't react in the next couple of seconds, he would pretend he was being bitten by something and casually remove it.

Meg leaned back against him with another small sigh. Her head was just under his chin, wisps of curly hair tickling his face, and suddenly it seemed perfectly natural for his arm to be around her, holding her. He grinned into the darkness. *McKendrick, you are such a jerk!*

"Meg," he said after a while. "Your dad drove me here tonight. You really got to him this time. He's a classic father, and you're his daughter, not his super-efficient, live-in housekeeper and general manager. Talk to him, Meg. Tell him you can't do—" Meg made a protesting sound, but he tightened his grip on her and went on. "All right, you *can* do all the work of keeping the house going and the chauffeuring and school and Cricket all by yourself, but you shouldn't have to. Your family needs someone like Mrs. B. Tell him, Meg. He's ready to listen."

"And if I don't, you will. Right?"

Oh lord . . . here we go. "Well yeah, except— Meg, on the way up here I told him a lot of things already. He wanted to know," Matt added quickly as he felt her stiffen. "Meg, listen, if there's one thing I've learned in all this, it's that if you need someone and they don't know you need them, you aren't doing them any favors by not telling them."

She thought about this for a long time. As she gradually relaxed under his arm, he decided it might be a good idea to change the subject.

"Hey," he whispered to the top of her head. "I've got something for you." Holding one of her hands palm up in his, he fished around in his pockets until he found what he wanted. Putting it into her hand, he closed her fingers over it. She opened them immediately to feel the small round disk on its chain.

"What is it—a St. Christopher medal?"

"No, it's a thing I won in a race when I was nine, but that's not important. I mean, that's not why I want you to have it. Meg, I've been a real pain in the ass. I've made life miserable for you and said a lot of things I wish I hadn't said and never told you thanks for all the great times, and—"

Meg giggled, a small faint chirp like one of Cat's. "Do you think we could have all that engraved on the back? Maybe somebody who puts the Lord's Prayer on the heads of pins could do it."

"You nut! How about just one word—sorry?"

"No. I don't mind hearing you say it once, but I don't

want that word hanging around my neck all the time. Let's leave it the way it is." She slipped it over her head. "Move your arm a second," she said, adjusting the chain under her hair. Before he could put it back, she shifted so she could slide one arm between his spine and the wall and the other across his chest, and clasp her arms together around him.

For a second her face was turned up to his. Go for it! he told himself. Swiftly, so lightly he hoped she might not have noticed, he kissed her. Before he had time to wonder whether he had gone too far, her arms tightened around him. "Thanks," she whispered.

He sighed himself. As the air left his lungs, contentment welled up from somewhere inside to fill the empty space.

"You know something?" Meg's muffled voice seemed to reach his ears by way of his rib cage and spinal column. "You would have liked my mother. She was a lot like you in some ways, always rushing in where ordinary mortals fear to tread." She made a small sound that could have been a laugh. "Like the time in the shopping center, remember? A boy tried to snatch an old lady's purse and you caught him and scared him half to death?" Matt grunted. "My mom did something like that once. She couldn't hang on to the boy, but she did get the purse back, and she went and visited the old lady in the hospital every day until she got out and went home." Meg sat up, stretching her cramped muscles before she leaned against Matt's shoulder. "I guess it's better to be a busybody than a nothing. At least people miss you when you're not around."

"I guess," he agreed, thinking of his own parents. It reminded him that their mission was not quite accomplished. "Ready to go? They're waiting for us."

"I guess." Meg sighed. "Thanks, fellow busybody. I feel a lot better."

"So do I."

Ryder's car was still out in front of the Schuylers' when they finally arrived. Meg walked in through the front door without hesitation, Matt a step or two behind. Everyone was in the family room, and Meg stopped in the doorway, turning back to Matt as silence fell. "Looks like a busybody convention," she said in a mischievous undertone.

Like a scene from a musical, the room behind her was suddenly filled again with sound and movement. Carey came up shyly and whispered something in Meg's ear. She had obviously been crying.

"Me too," Meg told her, and Carey sent Matt one of her brilliant smiles before she fled down the hall to her room.

No one else seemed inclined to leave. Matt felt a flicker of alarm. Meg would never talk to her father in front of a crowd like this.

"Can we go home?" he said, sending Sally a silent plea for help. She nodded, and under cover of the apologies and thanks and good-byes, Matt told Will to get himself and Lew out of there and leave Meg and her father alone. The last thing he saw was Meg's proud straight back unbending a little, and the slow smile that was replacing her father's uncertain expression as he reached for her.

29

Matt was ready for bed, his hand on the light switch, when it struck him that he had left one vital thing undone. He found Ryder and Sally in the library.

"Could I make a long distance call?"

"At this hour?" Ryder sounded doubtful. "Who would be enthusiastic about hearing from you at ten fifty-five p.m.?" He answered his own question. "Gary?"

"Yes. I want to ask him down for spring vacation if it's okay with you."

Sally exchanged a delighted glance with Ryder. "Of course it is, Matt. We'd love to have him."

There was a phone in the library, but he used the one in the kitchen in case things didn't work out. For several seconds after he finished dialing, he got no response and was about to start dialing again when somewhere between California and Idaho machinery clicked into place and the connection was made. Matt let out a huge sigh and realized he had been holding his breath.

"Yes?" Gary's father spoke abruptly into his ear.

Matt made his voice higher than normal. "Is Gary home?"

"Yes. Who is this?" Uncle Frank did not sound too pleased.

"Roger," Matt said, pulling the name out of nowhere. He did not want to hold things up talking to Uncle Frank right now.

"You realize what time it is?"

"Yes, sir. I'm sorry, but it's important."

Gary's dad dropped the receiver—in his mind's eye, Matt could see it dangling down the wall beside the back door—and went to get Gary. Matt had time to wonder whether there were any Rogers in Craigie before Gary spoke. He sounded as if he were only a couple of blocks away.

"Who is this?" Crossly. So there weren't any Rogers in Craigie.

Matt took a deep breath, feeling it would have to last him a while. "Who else would it be at this time of night?"

Faintly, "Matt?"

"Yeah—Matt. The one and only original variety, not that freak who turned up in Craigie last summer."

Gary was silent for too long. Matt's mind began racing frantically. What now? Is he getting the message, or do we have to start a whole new round of apologies and explanations?

Gary's next question caught him by surprise. "Did you get the medal?"

"Yeah. I gave it away." He heard Gary's quick intake of breath and added hastily, "—to someone I wanted to say I was sorry to."

221

"Matt, I'm really—"

"Wait a second, good buddy. You've had your chance at that routine. It's my turn now, and then, if you don't mind, I'd like to give that particular word a rest." He paused for a moment. Gary was waiting. "Sorry, Freckles."

Gary let out a laugh that was half squeak. "You wouldn't call me that if you weren't a good safe distance away!"

"Try me!" Matt challenged him instantly. "Come on down here spring vacation and just try me. That's an invitation, in case you haven't had one lately and don't know what they sound like."

"You mean it? Spring vacation? Wait a second!" The phone hit the wall with a crash. Matt could hear Gary's feet thumping into the distance and his voice yelling for his mom and dad. A minute later Matt heard him coming back, still yelling. "Yes . . . no . . . I guess so, he didn't say. Matt?" He was still shouting. Feeling like whooping and hollering himself, Matt held the phone a couple of feet from his ear for safety. "They say it's okay as long as I promise to come home when the week is up, and you promise not to drag me into any crazy scrapes, and—"

"Me? Drag you into scrapes?"

"—and it's okay with the Ryders, and Mom wants to hear from somebody officially, and she and Dad send you their you-know-what!"

"Okay, okay!" Matt was laughing so hard by this time he could barely hold up the phone, let alone his end of the conversation. Gary could imitate his mom's whirlwind style right down to the inflections.

"Well, I guess I'll see you around, Big Matt."

222

"Okay, Little Red."

"Man, you just wait until I get off that plane, you—!"

"I'll be there. Don't worry."

Silence fell between them suddenly like a wall of sound-proof glass. They had so much to tell each other, so much catching up to do, there was no use starting now.

"Well, I guess that's it," Gary said finally. "Have a great Christmas."

"Yeah. You too. See you, Gare." Matt hung up slowly, reluctant to cut the connection between them now that it had been restored. Remembering back, looking ahead—he felt so fantastically happy he had to share it with someone or burst.

Ryder looked up from his book as Matt appeared in the doorway. "All set?"

Sally laughed. "Can't you tell by his face, Les?"

Matt grinned at both of them. "He can come, but his mom wants official notice from somebody that it's all right."

"I'll write her first thing in the morning, Matt," Sally promised.

Matt leaned on the door jamb, looking at Sally's bent head, Ryder's strong profile. If you love me, he told them silently, even half as much as I love you—

"Is there something else, Matt?" Ryder sounded as if he were resigned to the inevitable. If it wasn't one thing, his tone said, it was probably another. Matt knew when he was being teased.

"No—nothing else." His grin widened mischievously as a thought struck him. Two could play at that game. "At

223

least, not right now. But I guess I'd better not make any promises about tomorrow."

In the second it took for this to sink in, Matt had faded from their sight. The warm, relaxed sound of their laughter followed him all the way down the hall to his room, promising that whatever tomorrow turned up in the way of times good, bad, or just fair-to-middling, they would all be living through it together.